Take Me to Texas

Carmody was once a respected lawman. Even now, when he is running from the law with his gang of desperadoes and is wanted in three counties for jailbreak and robbery, he can hardly believe how much things have changed.

He cannot forgive his former friend, Sheriff Reece Chandler, for putting him in jail . . . so once he has pulled off the biggest robbery in Whiplock's history, and before he flees to exile in Mexico, he vows to have his revenge!

By the same author

The Immortal Marshal
Get Dellinger
Two for Sonora
One Last Notch
Lobo
In the Name of the Gun
Last Mile to Nogales
Livin' Ain't Forever

Take Me to Texas

Ryan Bodie

ROBERT HALE · LONDON

First published in Great Britain 2009

ISBN 978-0-7090-8819-6

Robert Hale Limited
Clerkenwell House
Clerkenwell Green
London EC1R 0HT

www.halebooks.com

Typeset by
Derek Doyle & Associates, Shaw Heath
Printed and bound in Great Britain by
CPI Antony Rowe, Chippenham and Eastbourne

CHAPTER 1

ROPE PARTY

Wes Carmody had been called many things in his life – outlaw, gunfighter, rogue and renegade, but nobody had ever suggested he was stupid. Any man with a price on his head would have had to be mindless not to recognize the danger in what he saw that day upon glancing out of the side window of Natchez Flats's Three Deuces Saloon.

There were dark figures closing in from all sides.

Ominous in their stealthy silence and with the light of the dying day glinting off gunmetal, they came stalking from an alleyway and were making directly for the saloon. Carmody saw that one man was not carrying a weapon. Instead he had a heavy coil of yellow rope slung over his shoulder with one end fashioned into the shape of a hangman's noose.

Carmody had survived imprisonment and the life of an escapee on the outlaw trails of the south-west by virtue of leadership and gunspeed. A flick of the wrist sent the last of his rye whiskey down his throat; he swept up his hat and was easing out of the back door, all in a matter of moments.

The hulking leader of the Natchez Flats lynch pack turned grey with shock in the narrow backyard's gloom as the outlaw they had planned to surprise suddenly loomed directly before them. Carmody struck with the speed of a rattler.

One brutal punch dropped the towner in his tracks with blood trickling from his broken mouth as unconsciousness claimed him.

'He's out here at the back!' a hoarse voice shouted.

Carmody cleared the sagging rear fence in one giant leap and hit the ground running to make it safely to his horse before the first gunshot exploded with a roar like a siege cannon behind him.

The chestnut stallion cleared the rickety fence with ease and, urged on by its rider, stormed away down the shadowy street at a dead run.

Carmody had never encountered a horse to match his chestnut over a quarter mile. By the time he'd put that distance between him and the town, he could see that the tardy posse which came boiling out of town in his dust wasn't going to be able to run him down on this or any other night.

For, coupled with speed to burn, the stallion also possessed real staying power. The chasers, less expensively mounted or motivated, fell rapidly behind until within minutes they were gone from sight in the gloom and dust far behind him.

Carmody had deliberately taken the western trail from the dusty little Texas town. He continued to follow it further and further away from his secret hideout, but after an hour's swift riding and the posse shaken off, he turned and swung south-east again. The moon came up as he crossed a featureless plain and rode on steadily through the pallid light until the granite shapes of the Devil's Marbles loomed ahead.

Only now did rider and lathered horse slacken the pace.

The outlaw's eyes probed the pits of black moon shadow surrounding the great monolithic stone formations lying directly ahead of him where hidden eyes stared out at him.

'Who is it?' a disembodied voice challenged.

'Wes.'

Shapes emerged from the shadows; Creed's rugged silhouette first and lean Demmon close behind. Next the Yost twins and finally Old Shacker toting his sawed-off Richardson in the crook of his arm as carefully as you would a baby.

The outlaws looked hopeful as Carmody rode in. Pickings had been mighty lean of late and they hoped he was returning with a promising report on the express office in Natchez Flats they planned to plunder.

Hopes faded as soon as they saw just how beat and badly blown his big horse was. The condition of the animal and the grim set to Carmody's jaw as he stepped down told the story without words.

It had been another failure – another 'dry hole'.

Silence fell and the good spirits that had sustained the bunch during a long day's wait under a broiling sun evaporated as they trailed his tall figure into the campsite.

What had gone wrong? The silent faces demanded answers as he halted to tug off his riding gloves. Bad luck again? Surely they'd already had more than their share of that of late?

His terse nod confirmed their fears. He sighed, then related why the town had proven another failure. His summary was that west Texas was simply growing too dangerous, for somebody in Natchez Flats had recognized his well-publicized features and he'd been lucky to escape with a full hide.

The notion that the biggest state in the Union might be getting too small for them was a depressing thought, even for this hardcase bunch.

'Well, hell, ain't your fault what happened, Wes,' Jamie Yost opined after a strung-out silence. 'We'll just mosey on to the next town and try our luck there, is all.'

'There ain't another town in fifty lousy miles,' growled brother Ben. The Yost twins were both big and good-natured, brawling redheads.

'I'm talking to the butcher, not the block!' Jamie retorted, and violence would have exploded then and there had Creed not stepped between them.

'Hush up, crackbrains!' Creed rapped, and they wisely fell silent. The hardcase's voice came out of a powerful body and granite features. Creed was a brooding, black-haired Kansan with one of the fastest gun hands in the west. He turned to Carmody and his jaw was set hard. 'So, what next?'

He spoke with respect yet his voice carried an edge. There had been jobs which Creed believed they might have pulled off successfully had Carmody worried less about the safety of his henchmen. The tough Kansan was beginning to wonder if they could afford to be that squeamish any longer.

'Give the man time,' interjected Old Shacker, a leather-faced veteran with an upright carriage and a stubborn jawline.

'It just could be that time is running out, old man,' drawled lean Demmon.

He looked across at Carmody and put on that boyishly innocent Iowa farmboy smile that made him appear more like a college kid than a man with a five-hundred dollar bounty on his head.

'Like Jamie says, Wes, ain't your fault we're running on empty, man. But I reckon that by this time next week we might have to start in eating whatever we can shoot.' He grimaced. 'Hell of a note for a genuine hell-raising outfit like us, huh?'

Old Shacker snorted. Blindly loyal to Carmody, he resented it when they started griping, particularly in view of the fact that the bunch owed its very freedom to him. Their spectacular bust out from Territory Prison had been planned and executed down to the last detail by the leader.

If Shacker, the veteran, had his way he'd tell all the rest to go to hell and fend for themselves, but he was not running this outfit. Wes Carmody was.

The flare of a match briefly illuminated Carmody's features as he touched a brown-paper quirley into life. He drew deeply.

'There's one job I've been saving for a rainy day. . . .'

Suddenly everybody was paying attention.

'A big job, Wes?' Ben Yost asked eagerly.

'Big enough.' Carmody appeared casual as he paced slowly to and fro before them, but had never been further from it. 'A branch of the Cattleman's Bank; it should be easy pickings if we go about it the right way. Only thing, it's over the border in New Mexico and that'd mean we'd have to cut through the Rio Hondo Badlands to avoid the posses out searching for us.'

'So, what's a stretch of badlands to a ringy bunch of six-gun stallions like us, Wes?' Demmon grinned.

'Heard tell in Natchez Flats that the Clansmen have been raiding right across the Badlands recent,' Carmody felt obliged to inform them.

This was sobering, for those ghostly outlaw raiders boasted a wide and grisly reputation even by south-western standards.

Rip Creed spoke in his direct way: 'What might this job of yours be worth, Wes?'

'It's the only bank in fifty miles,' Carmody supplied. 'Services some big, close-lying cattle outfits that are strong enough to keep going despite the recent threat posed by the Clansmen. It's also got a mine. So I calculate that bank could hold maybe five thousand in its vault at any given time.'

'Five grand!' Yost gasped. 'That's more than we've took in a year!'

'Just a minute,' Creed cut in. 'If this set-up is so flush and juicy, how come it don't get robbed every other week, Wes?'

'I didn't say it would be easy,' Carmody replied, all brisk action now as he headed for the horses. 'Let's talk it over while we ride.'

They trailed out after him without a word of protest. The twins started in punching one another on the shoulder, a sign of exuberance. They could always tell when Carmody believed he was on to something big. By the time they had broken camp and were back on the trail the only ones not grinning with anticipation were Carmody, who never smiled, and Old Shacker.

Shacker regarded himself as the wise old man of the outfit. His expression was plainly doubtful as he moved his horse forward to draw level with the leader.

'This town,' he growled. 'It got a name?'

'I don't want any arguments just yet, old man. We will put in some miles first, then we can jawbone.'

The veteran's stubbled jaw turned rocky and his stare grew more suspicious.

'You gotta have a reason for being so coy, seems to me.'

'I'm too beat to argue, is all.'

'But—'

'All right, goddamnit! Knowing you, you'll nag all the way to the border. Just give me your word there'll be no arguments and I'll level with you.'

Old Shacker turned his head and spat. He hated conditions. 'All right, you got my word. What is the name of this town?'

'Whiplock.'

It took a moment for the significance of that name to register. When it did, Old Shacker's mouth gaped wide, but Carmody held up a silencing hand.

'You gave your word. Now, shut your trap and ride.'

Shacker compressed stubbled lips and watched his leader kick on ahead into the deep Texan night. Slowly he reached for his chaw tobacco and bit off a generous chunk.

It didn't help him relax any.

For with the windswept vastness of the Rio Hondo Badlands and Whiplock their objective, Old Shacker couldn't help but wonder how desperate Carmody must be even to consider robbing a bank in a town whose formidable sheriff was the former friend of Carmody's whom he now hated worse than anybody in the west.

As it was prone to do – in that section of New Mexico bordering both Texas and the Rio Grande – the mercury had plummeted on sundown. There was a chill in the air of Whiplock as Sheriff Reece Chandler made his way back to the jailhouse after supper.

Men lounged in groups along the plankwalks of the central block, some leaning against the saloon fronts or perched on the racks where their horses were tied.

They were quiet tonight and spoke in low voices. Here and there amongst them the quick spurt of a vesta or the orange glow of a lighted cigarette showed in the gloom. Most were yarning amiably and there were few signs of the drunkenness or aggression which had almost destroyed the town here in the bad old days before Chandler pinned on the star.

Cynics might claim Whiplock was still a mean and

violent place underneath. They were likely right. But so long as that wild streak remained suppressed that was just fine both by Whiplock and its iron-fisted peace officer.

Most workers here were either miners or cowboys. Several nodded as the lawman passed, a few spoke, but most remained silent. Chandler was popular with the townsmen, but was widely resented by the troublemakers due to the two-fisted style of authority he enforced.

Still quiet for a paynight, the husky lawman mused as he passed the Plains Hotel. Too bad it wouldn't stay that way, and it certainly wouldn't with the crews in from the Double X taking on freight heavy at the Devilrider and Can-Can Saloons. And now the miners from the Sister Clara were beginning to arrive by wagon to swell the troublemakers' numbers too.

The lawman walked on, neither quickly nor slowly, a tall and broad-shouldered man with a challenging eye that could cower even a hell-raising cowhand. Or, mostly, that is. No lawman ever batted one hundred in places like Whiplock.

The man who had largely tamed this place dispensed an old-fashioned brand of law most often enforced with either fists or a six-gun barrel, but it worked.

Chandler's term of office had seen the brawling cowtown transformed into a solid community boasting two hotels, five saloons, a regular stage line, thriving business enterprises and a bank.

His many critics claimed that the cost of such improvement came at too high a price in terms of individual freedoms. And it was true that, whenever freedom threatened to become excess, Reece Chandler could prove a mighty hard man indeed.

Turning into the law office, the sheriff encountered his deputy emerging from the cells.

'Evening, Sheriff.'

'Mr Briggs.'

It was always, 'Sheriff' and 'Mr Briggs' between the lawmen despite the fact that lean and tough Briggs had worked under Chandler since the day of his appointment in Whiplock. The sheriff regarded his deputy as the best sidekick in the game, but conceded that Luther Briggs would always be a difficult and unpopular man. This deputy believed in his iron fists and Sheriff Chandler, but very little else.

'Anything happen while I was at supper, Mr Briggs?'

The deputy jerked a thumb over his shoulder. 'Prisoner Tolan turned down his chow at supper, but I persuaded him to eat it.'

The ghost of a smile touched Chandler's lips as he hung his hat on a peg. Briggs 'persuasion' could be a tad rough, particularly where brawling cowhands were concerned. And Wild Mick Tolan dearly loved a good knuckle-up.

'Anything else?'

'Some mail came in on the sun-down stage. A letter from Cracker Creek advises that a wagon got wiped out down at Jubal – three men killed. Miners. They reckon it could have been Clansmen.'

The sheriff grunted as he sat at his desk. Mostly the worst trouble in the wasteland regions at this time of year was caused by Clansmen. It was this season when the brigands were at their most active all across the Rio Hondo Badlands, robbing and pillaging then freighting their plunder down from Texas, across the Rio Grande and into Mexico.

The marauders tended to shy clear of closely settled regions like Whiplock County, but their attacks elsewhere were as frequent and murderous as ever this summer.

'Hmm.' The sheriff stroked his jaw. 'Maybe we'll take a patrol east and check out the Jimcrack Hills next week, Mr Briggs.'

'Whatever you say, Sheriff.'

Chandler looked up, sensing the man was holding something back.

'Anything else, Mr Briggs?'

Briggs cleared his throat. 'A note from the marshal at Fort Clanton, Texas; it seems there's been a sighting of Wes Carmody around Natchez Flats.'

The sheriff's stare sharpened instantly.

From time to time word on the Carmody gang sifted down to the border country from the north. Such reports never left the sheriff unmoved. For it was Chandler, then the sheriff of Hannibal, Northwest Texas, who had arrested Carmody for robbery; Chandler's arrest of his former friend had begun one of the most notorious outlaw careers in that part of the country.

The outlaw had been sentenced to five years hard labour in the Texas State Penitentiary, but Carmody had crashed out after just ten days with a bunch of inmates and had been leading the law of three states and territories a frustrating chase ever since.

From the very first, Carmody strenuously claimed Chandler had framed him and vowed to avenge this alleged injustice. Indeed, the outlaw had protested his innocence so convincingly that the trial judge had sentenced him to five years instead of the customary ten prescribed by law in such cases, almost as though he might have been halfway convinced of the accused's innocence.

The case had not affected Chandler's fine record, however. Yet the sheriff himself had always privately regarded the whole incident as a black mark against his name, something unsettled. He felt the judge's ambivalence at the Carmody trial had rubbed off on to others. Even here in Whiplock, where his respect was assured, the name of Carmody came up every now and again, often accompanied by speculative glances and the unspoken question: had Wes Carmody really been guilty or was he framed?

At length Chandler rose and moved to the big

map of the south-west which covered a section of the wall by the rifle rack. It took some time to locate the tiny pin prick on the map that was Natchez Flats. He continued to brood over the map until the sound of a match being scratched into life caused him to turn and see the deputy lighting up his pipe.

Dour and rugged, Briggs was not a heavy user of tobacco. In fact the sheriff knew the man rarely smoked his pipe other than when tense, and it took a lot to make him so.

The sheriff nodded. 'Mr Briggs, you're not thinking Carmody could be heading this way?'

'Reckon he'd have more horse sense than to do that.'

'So do I.' A pause, then, 'Although there would be nothing to stop him doing so, legally, considering the fact he has a clean slate here in New Mexico.'

'Nothin',' the deputy agreed. 'And more's the pity. I hope to live to see the day when fugitive warrants blanket the whole south-west, not just parts here and parts there, like a dog's breakfast.'

They might have said more, but for the sudden racket erupting from the cells; there was a curse and a crash, followed by sounds of violence.

'Tolan and Blaine at it again,' Briggs growled. He made for the archway but the sheriff held up his hand.

'I'll attend to it, Mr Briggs. It's past your supper time.'

Briggs just grunted and ambled out with the shotgun cradled in his arm. The uproar spilling from the cells indicated the cowboys were well and truly at it, no holds barred. Yet Chandler remained standing beneath the light staring at the map for a long half-minute further before turning away thoughtfully to go on through the archway. Upon reaching the cells he found Mick Tolan busily bashing Stacey Blaine's rock-hard skull against the brick wall.

The sheriff of Whiplock ordered the brawlers to desist instead of separating them with a pistol-whipping – a sure sign that rugged Chandler's mind was not on his job.

CHAPTER 2

NIGHT OF THE CLANSMEN

They were up there on the ridge.

Prospector Coley Beaumont knew it even before he hipped around in his saddle. It felt as if a chill wind had suddenly blown against his back.

Yet there was no hint of a breeze as the crimson sunset flooded the sky above the trail the leathery old-timer had been following east. For the cold wind that Coley Beaumont had felt was actually the chill of fear – the sudden realization that he never should have set out impatiently across the Rio Hondo Badlands alone, knowing the risks as he did.

His eyes, faded by years of sun and distance, scanned the ridge. It was empty. He glanced away, clenched his eyes, then turned back to look again. In those brief moments six grey-garbed horsemen mounted upon sturdy Texas mustangs had appeared in total silence and were seated on their ponies silhouetted against the fierce crimson sky.

The prospector was as tough as any old desert rat must be to have survived in this unmapped hell country of south-west Texas. In his time he'd fought the Apaches, Comanches, bandits, renegades and the natural savagery of the elements, yet was still alive and still boasted a full head of hair at sixty-one years of age. Yet tough and gutty as he was, the oldster blanched now as he sat his mule with the silent seconds slipping by, knowing only too well who these ghost riders were.

Clansmen!

It was a name that breathed terror all the way from the Texas Panhandle to deep into Old Mexico. These ghostly marauders had been ranging and raiding unfettered across the endlless tracts of semi-desert badlands since first emerging from the trackless emptiness of the Staked Plains back in Houston's day, and still largely dominated the wastelands thirty years later.

They raided the outlying ranches and villages of West Texas, slaughtered at will, then ran their blood-stained booty all the way down into Mexico in their swaying, two-wheeled carts or carretas to trade for gold.

So elusive were they in some regions, that many Texans believed them to be a myth. They had consistently evaded both army and law over the decades, often vanishing totally during the bitter Texan winters only to reappear in high summer to attack any who still dared venture out here beyond the protection of the law.

Beaumont had sighted them or their sign often enough – a line of grey riders crossing a moonlit plain, or the deep wheel tracks they left behind, cut by the wheels of their carretas. But he had never yet sighted the marauders at close range before, and he knew of nobody who had done so and lived to tell of it.

He slammed heels against horsehide and the mule jogged off in a shuffling walk-trot.

The horsemen lining the ridge watched him with the dying light glinting from crossed ammunition bandoleers and bristling weapons. Some wore huge Mexican sombreros, others flat-brimmed stetsons. There was about them an almost tangible aura of evil as though they might well be some miscegenation of the human gene. There were places in the southwest where the mere whisper of the word Clansmen! could touch off a panic and drive honest people to quit their homes to hide out in the wilds just in case the alarm should prove valid.

But they were as real as Death here this summer's night. . . .

The leader of this wolf pack seated astride his paint pony was hatless, with wild black hair tumbling to his shoulders.

Ten miles south lay Kruger's camp comprising thirty Clansmen, a pack of Indians and six carretas piled high with plunder and five white hostages being held for ransom. The band had been roving north in search of a smaller bunch of badland wanderers and had cut the prospector's trail simply by chance.

This grizzled old desert rat they had encountered didn't appear as if he would have two white dimes to rub together, but with prospectors, one never knew.

The marauders allowed him to travel a short distance further before starting down off the ridge, alkali dust boiling up from hard pony hoofs. They did not shout nor raise their weapons but came on swiftly in deliberate, chilling silence.

He kicked the mule hard and it reluctantly broke into a clumsy run. The Clansmen loped along comfortably behind. Beaumont wore no spurs. So he tied into his mount with hands and heels but the critter was incapable of genuine speed.

Finally the manhunters broke their silence, their mocking laughter rising to reach out to the old man, engulfing him. To them this was just a familiar game – the game of death.

Quickly, easily, they drew abreast.

'Old *hombre*, why do you use the mule with such

cruelty, eh?'

Then another voice from his opposite side; 'So, gringo, is it sociable to run like a dog when you meet fellow travellers of the trails, no?'

Beaumont's shaggy head jerked wildly around. He realized one of the horsemen was an American, a blond-headed kid of around eighteen with half his teeth missing and yellow eyes like a wild dog. An Americana – most likely a Texan – riding with these human wolves! Suddenly enraged, Beaumont clawed for the old Dragoon model Colt .44 riding on his hip. As the weapon came up, Kruger, riding off to one side, shot him in the back.

He fell. As he plunged to earth, the killer's weapon spewed smoke and flame again and the mule propped and also went down as if crashing into an invisible wall. With dust boiling high and enveloping the scene, the gray riders reined in and leaped down. They now holstered their guns and drew long-bladed knives.

It took a long time for Coley Whitmont to die.

Before this happened he was reduced to a whimpering, babbling hulk begging for death – something less than a man.

They located his gold straight off then performed a savage dance brandishing treasure and crimson blades aloft as they circled what had once been a human being, this ritual enacted to one of the most chilling sounds to be heard anyplace in the Rio

Hondo Badlands, the eerie, haunting music of the Clansmen flutes.

When they'd tired of the ritual, they assembled in a ragged circle to chant the victory song of the Clansmen – masters of life and death.

The sun fell swiftly as the pack rode off, but in the brief twilight before full darkness came, eagle eyes glimpsed the smudge of smoke hazing the south-eastern skyline.

Kruger raised a hand to bring the pack to a halt. For a time there was no sound but the creak of leather and the noisy blowing of the mustangs. The raiders continued to stare fixedly away over the scrubby hills at that silent drift of white in the sky.

'Trinity Creek,' the leader ascertained at length. 'I think somebody camps.'

'Someone who is maybe loco crazy in the head?' a big-nosed rider suggested.

Heads bobbed in agreement. The Clansmen had been raiding widely across the untamed regions for several weeks. Nobody in the vicinity could help but be aware of the raiders' presence by this. A stubborn prospector might occasionally still attempt to sneak his way across, travelling only by night and hiding like a dog coyote by daylight, but surely only a blind fool would announce his presence by lighting a campfire?

Kruger turned his scarred face south.

He'd planned to overnight at Camp Creek then at

first light follow their ancient trail south across the Rio Bravo and back into Mexico. Men and mounts needed a solid night's rest against the long miles ahead.

When he saw the eager unasked question in their eyes, he was negative and firm. 'We do not have time . . . we must rest. That smoke is far from here.'

'Hell, chief,' protested the ugly young American, 'Trinity Creek ain't no more'n two hours ride from here. We could mosey over and take a look-see, at least. Could be worth our while?'

Kruger considered. It was plain every man was eager for more action, the possibility of more blood and plunder. His authority was unchallenged, yet he was always wise enough not to deny them a reasonable request, particularly when their blood was up.

He reached a decision quickly.

'*Sí*, you may ride to the creek, but you will return by midnight.'

With a wild yippee the young American slapped his pony with his hat and raced away at full gallop, the others following hard behind. Kruger watched their figures recede swiftly into the twilight haze with an indulgent smile. His children, he told himself, his brutal, high-spirited brothers of the blood.

He touched his horse with steel and rode south alone for Camp Creek as the Texas moon climbed the sky to drench the earth with a gentle yellow light.

*

The flame of sunset dimmed across the badlands; dusk was creeping through the gaunt willows and sickly sycamores lining Trinity Creek as the six horsemen rode in to make camp. A crane cleared the water and winged off downstream and a cottontail hopped into a hollow log.

That was the rabbit's first mistake, for these were hungry men with long miles behind them. Its second error came when it erupted from the log under the prod of a sharp stick to be neatly bagged in young Jamie Yost's hat.

A one-handed chop and one Rio Hondo jackrabbit was ready to be cleaned and eaten. The only query remaining was whether it was to be consumed cooked or raw.

'Raw,' grunted Carmody, offsaddling the stallion.

'Aw shucks, Wes,' protested Ben Yost, 'we had jerky for nooners and leftover raw fish for breakfast. Ain't it high time we had some cooked vittles?'

'You light a fire here and most likely what will get to be cooked up will be our goose.'

'Wes is right, Ben,' chimed in Old Shacker, grunting as he dragged his heavy Texan saddle off his horse's sweating back. 'Hell, boy, you seen that Clansmen sign just as plain as we all did.'

'Clansmen!' Yost snorted contemptuously. 'Why, the last time I tangled with one of them greyguts he wound up wearing his ugly head back-to-front!'

Ben Yost was not bragging. Some time back the bunch had clashed with a Clansmen raiding party, with fatal results for the vermin. But that had been just one small party riding the very outer limits of the raiders' range. This was different. Tonight, the gang was deep in the heart of the Rio Hondo badlands, and they had cut enough sign to know that the Clansmen were thick on the ground in these parts right now.

'We eat raw or we don't eat at all,' Carmody said with an air of finality.

'I don't fancy eating raw meat again.'

The speaker was Rip Creed. The Kansan gunman stood leaning against his horse with a dead match jutting between his teeth and deep furrows cutting leathery cheeks. Creed was a hard man, possibly the hardest in the bunch. He was certainly fastest with a Colt .45. He did not readily accept leadership from another, for in essence he was a loner with a gunfighter's touchy pride. He didn't get along with the serious Carmody, and yet had followed him loyally and with lethal distinction over several long months, for, despite his toughness and lethal talents, Rip Creed was no leader whereas Carmody was born for the role.

Carmody didn't respond immediately. He toted his saddle across to a tree, dumped it, then returned to his horse with a rub-down rag and began swabbing lather from the stallion's flanks.

The others were waiting to see how this played out. Their attitudes were mixed. Shacker, Demmon and the Yosts were all loyal to Wes, yet were also very hungry.

Finally Carmody turned to stare directly at Creed, but before he could speak, Old Shacker stepped forward.

'Wes,' he drawled, 'it wouldn't take long to cook up one cottontail, you know.'

Carmody put a sharp stare on him. 'Who asked you, old man?'

Shacker grinned. 'You know me, Wes. I can't keep my mouth closed any more than can a big-mouth bass. You've said so yourself. Often. We got long miles behind us and longer ones ahead, and likely we need proper fuelling up if we're to make it.'

Shacker was sober then. None knew if he was really ready to risk lighting a fire, or simply wanted to head off conflict between the two deadliest shootists in the bunch.

Long seconds slid by. Carmody exhaled, and finally relented.

'All right, but make sure you set the fire with willow sticks. They raise the least smoke.'

Relief – you could almost smell it!

The twins yipped in unison and immediately began darting about gathering up kindling sticks. Demmon produced his blade and set about dressing their catch. Finally Old Shacker winked at Carmody and returned to his off-saddling. Creed ambled across to the leader, still chewing on his match.

'No hard feelings, Wes?'

'Hell no, man. You go stand first watch.'

Creed's face darkened instantly. 'Why me?'

Wes swung to face him. 'Because I say so.'

'What if I say go to hell?'

Carmody rested his saddle on the stallion's withers and turned to face the bigger man squarely again.

'Why don't you say it and see how it plays out?'

The fire-building ceased. The skinning knife paused above a half-stripped carcass. Old Shacker swallowed so drily you could hear it.

'You're bracing me, Wes?' Creed asked in a thick voice.

'Call it what you crave.'

Their eyes locked and held each other's gaze. Creed's stare was unreadable, but it was plain to all Carmody would not give ground. The bigger man began to fidget under that steady stare, and finally kicked at a rock and cursed.

'Hell, no call to get all riled up, Wes.'

'No call at all. Go take the first watch. I'll take the second.'

Creed scooped up his rifle and moved off for the low hill on the south side of the camp. Everybody started breathing easier once again.

By the time Carmody was finished with his mount

the campfire crackled merrily and the fragrant aroma of cooking rabbit filled the air. Shacker had set the coffee pot beside the flames while the twins, genuinely excited by the prospect of hot food, were all over the site, only pausing occasionally to thump one another playfully with blows that might have put lesser men on the critical list.

'She's not making much smoke, Wes,' remarked Demmon as Carmody joined him at the fire.

'Scarce any,' Carmody agree, hunkering down. 'Good-looking rabbit.'

Demmon grunted in agreement, a lean and hard-bitten fellow who gave the impression of always holding himself on a leash. The man was solid and reliable – so long as he stayed sober. Put outside a skinful of rye whiskey however, he could be as unpredictable as a Texan twister and twice as dangerous.

'Good as you'd get anyplace,' he affirmed, turning the carcass with a green stick. 'But wild rabbit'll be real rough eating compared with what we'll be wolfing down soon, eh, Wes?'

'I reckon.'

'Will we be heading for Old Mex after this job?'

'Yeah. We just need one good haul to take to Mexico with us.'

'What then?'

'What do you mean?'

'Well, I've had me a feeling for quite a spell that

you just might be tiring of the life, Wes. Had a hunch if we made the big killing you might just up and quit . . . mebbe.'

'Could do at that.'

'Go back to ranching?'

Carmody's features softened as he picked up a burning stick to touch his cheroot into life. He was country born and bred and had never lost his love of the land.

'A man could do worse. How about you, Abe?'

'Reckon I could make you a ranchhand?'

'If you kept away from hard liquor . . . most likely.'

'If,' Abe Demmon sighed. 'That sure is one hell of a Jim Dandy big word, ain't it?' He turned the rabbit again, nodded. 'Say, I reckon this here cottontail has to be about ready.'

'Won't get any readier,' Carmody affirmed. He turned. 'OK, come and get it, boys!'

It was a fine meal, even though portions were small. They ate with relish, washing down chunks of meat with hot coffee. The fire was doused immediately, yet it took some time for the last feathery tendrils of smoke to disappear. Too long, as it turned out.

They were still licking their fingers and draining the last of the coffee when Creed hustled down from his look-out position to announce the approach of horsemen.

'How many?' Carmody demanded, uncoiling to

his feet.

'Five, I make it,' replied Creed. 'Just could be Clansmen, by the looks.' The big man's jaws worked. 'Maybe I was wrong about that fire after all, man.'

'Forget it. How far away?'

'Not far. They came though that brushy arroyo. They were drawing close when I sighted them.'

'Not much point in us high-tailing it on played-out horses,' Carmody replied. He hesitated a moment, then said, 'We'll make a stand here. Ben, start the fire up again.'

Yost blinked. 'Start the fire?'

'Don't give me jaw, man. Just do what I say!'

'Whatever you say, boss.'

Within minutes the campsite was deserted except for the single, red-shirted figure squatted before the crackling campfire. Carmody smoked a short cigar and stared into the flames. He grew aware of a faint rustling in the brush and, above the smell of the smoke detected the wild, gamey whiff of unwashed bodies. He poked at the fire and smoke trickled lazily from his lips. A finger of wind dipped out of the sky and lifted a gust of powdery ash from the fire and dusted it across his bedroll. His horse stirred nervously, turning its head southwards, the fire reflected in the moist jewels of its eyes.

Time passed and Carmody flicked the butt into glowing coals.

Then the vagrant breeze came up again, and as though boosted by its strength five grey-clad figures ghosted from the trees into the light.

The Clansmen wore no spurs, nothing that might jingle and give them away. Firelight sheened off naked gun barrels and burnished brown faces alike with an orange sheen. The fire popped as they halted, staring at the solitary figure. They thought he looked prosperous, and that big chestnut stallion would certainly be a valuable prize.

A hairy-faced hellion named Gomez cocked his big .44. At the sound of the click, Carmody turned and stared at them. They expected a shocked reaction, yet he surveyed them as calmly as if they were so many harmless fat businessmen he was encountering upon the main street of San Antonio. Black-bearded Gomez stepped forward, brandishing his cocked .45.

'Reach!' he snapped.

Carmody did not blink. 'I've got a better notion, scum. You reach – or die!'

The Clansman blinked. Something was very wrong here. Either this lone gringo had no notion who they were, or else he was loco.

The sunken-chested hellion with a face like a knife blade stepped into sight from behind Gomez. 'You stand next to death and you dare call on us to surrender—'

'That's what the man said.'

The disembodied voice floated from the deep shadows beyond the fireglow towards the tiny creek. It came clear as a gunshot from behind a deadfall log. Jerking around in that direction, the hellions caught the wink of light reflecting from gun metal.

'Drop your weapons, scum!' Carmody ordered, uncoiling to his feet and palming a six-shooter. 'We've got you cold!'

The order packed enough authority to cause Gomez to drop his piece, and saw the second hellion begin to shake and back up, but all it did to the flat-faced American in the faded blue shirt was to galvanize him into anger – and action.

He whipped up his gun and triggered wildly. Instantly scarlet gunflashes reached out for him from the shadows. He clutched at his chest with both hands and bright crimson bubbled through his fingers. Carmody's Colt joined in the sixgun chorus and the outlaw went spinning away with a sudden third eye in the centre of his forehead.

As Carmody hurled his body to one side, the volley from the shadows became a vicious scythe of murderous lead that chopped the killers down in their tracks. Instantly Gomez went crashing backwards with his skull bursting open like a ripe melon. A short distance from where he fell another was buckling as he fell with convulsions causing him to jerk trigger and pump shots harmlessly into the earth at his feet.

The surviving Clansman, a youthful beanpole with yellow eyes bugging in terror, sprang for the sanctuary of the trees. A fusillade of shots chopped him down. He managed to get up bloodily, staggered two more steps only to be sent flying again as the raging guns homed in on him. For a third, incredible time he somehow made it back to his feet, but he was a walking dead man who only required one further bullet to hurl his dead body into the shadows.

The gap-toothed American had struggled to his knees with his Colt still in his fist. Beneath the cover of fogging gunsmoke, he squeezed trigger and a leaden wasp flicked Carmody's black hair. Retaliatory fire spurted from the trees and the Clansman fell on his face, kicking at the ground.

Silent and grim the outlaws slowly emerged from the timber. Finally the tow-head's death convulsions ceased. The gun echoes were fading off into the night, brushed away by a gentle wind.

'Idjuts!' Old Shacker muttered. 'Why didn't they quit when they had the chance? A blind fool could see they never had a prayer.'

There was regret in the veteran's voice, for Shacker was a man who genuinely hated to take life, even the lives of scum like this. His reaction was reflected in the faces of Carmody, the Yost twins, even Abe Demmon. For these were men who regarded themselves as outlaws only by necessity, not inclination; they refused to see themselves as killers. Only Rip Creed appeared pleased with the results. This was a man who could kill without compunction.

'You all right, Wes?' Ben Yost asked after a silence.

Carmody fingered the back of his head, studied a bullet-clipped clump of hair a moment, then nodded.

'That was kinda risky, you sitting decoy like you done, Wes,' Jamie remarked.

'It worked, didn't it?' Carmody countered.

'Like a charm,' Creed drawled. 'Just like a gold-plated charm.'

Abe Demmon fingered fresh shells into his piece with practised ease. 'Well, that's five of the scum that won't get to murder little kids or rape good women again.' He closed the gun with a snap. 'Good day's work.'

Heads nodded in silent agreement. Carmody slowly circled the fire. The faces of the death were ashen in the moonlight, mouths gaping, teeth snarling silently, jaws locked. He turned his back and stared at the moon. When he spoke his voice was not quite steady.

'Let's just get to hell and gone away from here.'

'Are we riding then, Wes?' asked Old Shacker.

Carmody didn't answer straight off, his expression thoughtful as he stood a little distance apart. None knew that for the past two weeks he had been leading them southwest with a particular destination in mind: a hard-knuckle mining town with a formidable sheriff.

Carmody had business in that town, yet gazing about at both the dead and the grim and weary faces of his friends, he suddenly realized they were in no shape for pushing on to that destination right now. Rather they should rest up some and get themselves into shape for what lay ahead, namely the most dangerous job the gang had pulled in their months together.

He recalled a remote backwoods quarter they'd passed by some days earlier, well off the beaten track but quiet and peaceful-looking. He'd remembered the name – Pinewood Range.

'We're on our way,' he announced. And, hoisting his big Spanish-Texan saddle off the ground, strode away towards his horse.

CHAPTER 3

THE CLANSMEN

Ma Jenner stared at the battered old clock on the sideboard with disgust. Here it was gone nine on a sunny morning and not one blessed thing accomplished about the place other than those chores she and Marylou had performed in the kitchen!

'I declare,' she complained, slamming the coffee pot down on the glowing lid of the ancient, pot-bellied stove, 'if energy was gunpowder they wouldn't be able to muster enough of the stuff between them all to blow a chicken off a buffalo chip.'

'They' were the menfolk of the remote, hard-scrabble Cross H Ranch – namely Pa Jenner and son Tommy. The ranch was thirty miles east of Whiplock in the Pinewood Range and a thousand miles from prosperity. It never ceased to amaze Ma that two mortal men who, by her standards, did so very little, could possibly get so tired doing it. To Ma, six in the morning was sinfully late, and if a body wasn't up and about by seven it was scarce worth getting up at all.

'Well, they did patch the corral fence yesterday, Ma,' the girl reminded her mother. Marylou Jenner had long given up on her father, but invariably took her brother's part. 'Now, didn't they?'

'Maybe so. But only after I'd nagged myself blue in the face,' she recalled. 'And even then they didn't finish the chore proper.'

'The corral looks all right to me, Ma,' Marylou said, gazing from the window.

'Yeah? Well, you just wait until Juniper gets to test it out,' Ma grumbled. Juniper was the ranch mule, the laziest worker, but mightiest kicker in the county. The feud between animal and tetchy matriarch was a local legend.

'You won't nag Tommy about the work, will you, Ma?' Marylou begged. 'He really did his best.'

Ma's honest, apple-cheeked face, marked and seamed prematurely by two decades of care, hard work and struggle, softened as she studied her daughter. There was little in this woman's life to be happy about, but Marylou was the sun that warmed her. Just eighteen years of age, and as shyly pretty as a fawn, the girl was everything a daughter should be, and more, in her mother's eyes. Ma knew she would never rest until they had gotten away from here and she had seen Marylou set up all legally wed to some fine gentleman who would treat her like a princess for the rest of her life.

'Sit down and have a cup of coffee with me, honey,' she sighed. 'We've earned it even if nobody else on this place has.'

Mother and daughter sat in the morning sunlight streaming through the open window on to the bare boards of the floor. There was no linoleum on the floors yet they were immaculately clean. From deeper within the unpainted little frame house drifted the faint sounds of snoring that mingled with the chittering of the morning birds in the tree outside.

'Collected three eggs this morning, Ma.'

'That's fine, honey.'

'And got two ripe pumpkins.'

'Good girl.'

'And I broke my ankle climbing up to the barn loft.'

'That's nice, dear.'

Marylou smiled. 'Ma, you're not listening to a blind word I say. What are you thinking about?'

It was a rhetorical question. For Marylou Jenner knew exactly what occupied her mother's thoughts whenever she got that faraway look in her still handsome eyes. She was thinking of a green place down in Mexico where the grass was lush, the water plentiful, where all that was needed was a little work to build the sort of place the Cross H could never become. Ma was thinking of her tract of land down at San Robles in Chuchilo County, left to her by a kinsman recently, yet only theirs if and when they might work up the courage to challenge the thirty-mile strip of the Rio Hondo Badlands they must cross if they ever wanted to get there.

She sighed wearily and glanced towards the bedrooms. 'Just day-dreaming, honey. . . .'

Marylou reached out and touched her hand. 'It's not a day-dream, Ma. You mustn't ever start believing it is. We'll get there someday soon, and Mexico will prove even better than you dreamed. Just wait and see.'

Ma's bosom heaved again.

'How long does a body have to wait for a boy to turn into a man, Marylou? Every birthday Tommy has, I look at him and shake my head and say . . . "Next year, mebbe he will—" '

She broke off at the sudden braying erupting outside. 'Glory be! What is that infernal animal raising hell about this time?'

'Probably just the rooster tormenting him again, Ma. Come on, drink up your coffee and stop fretting so. You'll worry yourself sick one day.'

They talked on, disregarding the racket from outside as the mule continued to raise hell. It didn't occur to either woman that the animal's braying might herald the arrival of visitors.

Nobody ever stopped by Cross H Ranch.

Not only was the ranch spread ten miles off the main trail and on the fringe of the San Robles Badlands, but the hard-luck Jenners had no real friends and received few visitors. Drummers and panhandlers knew there was no point wasting time and energy going there in search of either a sale or a hand-out. Whatever cash the clan ever came by, Ma salted away against the big day they would pack up and travel the south-west badlands . . . if they dared.

Their last visitor was Sam, the Walking Preacher, who showed up one dismal morning four months back to do a little praying over them then stayed on and almost ate them out of house and home before Pa chased him off with a charge of bird shot from his pea rifle.

Tommy Jenner finally appeared, yawning and stuffing his shirt tail into his corduroys.

'Morning, Ma, Sis? That coffee I smell?'

'You mean midday coffee, don't you?' Ma said critically. Then her face softened and she hustled across to the stove. 'Sorry sweetie, I'm a bit tetchy this morning. Ask your sister. Go on, go feed your chickens and I'll fix you some vittles.'

As the girl went out a slender boy with a shock of fair hair and a handsome face marred only by a weak chin, Tommy Jenner dropped into his chair and stretched luxuriously. He frowned as he lowered his arms, glancing at the doorway.

'What's eating that goddamned jackass?'

'Tommy!' chided Ma. 'Language!'

'Sorry, Ma. But what's wrong with him anyway? Woke me in the middle of a big dream, so he did.'

'Your daddy awake yet, son?'

'Snoring like a buzz-saw when I came by his door, Ma. . . .'

The boy broke off sharply. Ma waited for him to continue, before realizing he was staring open-jawed at the doorway. Ma's hand flew to her breast. A man stood framed in the doorway with one hand resting against the frame and the sunlight outlining his tall, well-made physique. They had never seen him before, yet one glance was all Ma needed to know beyond any doubt that whoever he might be, and whatever had brought him here, it added up to one thing: trouble.

Wes Carmody mounted the back porch and touched the door with his rifle barrel, pushing it inwards. From the front he could hear Creed's deep voice reassuring someone that everything would be just fine providing everybody acted sensibly. Much closer at hand Carmody could hear the sounds of snoring and the creak of bedsprings.

He turned to stare across the ranchyard. The twins were over by the corrals with their rifles while

Demmon checked out the barn. He nodded silently to Old Shacker and they entered the cabin from the rear and made directly for the first bedroom door.

A man lay sprawled on his back on an old fourposter with his mouth wide open, snoring like a buzz-saw. He came awake fast when a rifle muzzle jabbed him in the ribs to see two gun-toting strangers standing by his bedside.

'Up!' Carmody ordered. 'This is no time for an honest man to be in bed anyway.'

Pa Jenner made a croaking sound in his throat and went hobbling from the room in his long johns. Shacker trailed him through to the kitchen while Carmody checked out the remaining rooms. Ma Jenner had almost recovered from her initial shock by the time Carmody entered the kitchen behind her husband and Old Shacker.

'Outlaws!' she shouted, standing by the stove with a cook pot in her hand. 'Pa, do something!'

Pa Jenner didn't move a muscle. It was all he could do to breathe. He hadn't been so scared since Sam Caleb had threatened to cut off his credit at the whiskey still on Buzzard Hill.

Contempt etching her features, Ma transferred her attention to her son. 'Tommy, go get the rifle!'

'Ma'am,' Old Shacker said, removing his hat, 'would you like to hush up a moment and let us explain what we're doing here?'

'Don't soft-soap me, you ragged old ruffian!' Ma

said stoutly. She waved her pot threateningly. 'I'm not afraid of your rotten, thieving kind!'

They believed her. So Shacker put on his best smile. 'Ma'am, we mean you and your folks no harm. Honest Injun.'

'Oh no, sure you don't.' The woman's tone was bitterly sarcastic. 'Gun-toting hellions bust in on peaceful, law-abiding folks, and they don't mean to harm nobody. Tell us another!'

'Six, Ma,' Tommy said from the window.

'What?'

'There's three more outside.'

Ma slowly lowered her pot. Three outlaws packing weapons she might be able to deal with. But six. . . ?

Carmody crossed the room to the wide window, his body moving easily under the blood-red shirt. 'Just the four of you folks here?' he asked.

'That's so,' Tommy replied. The boy didn't appear scared as he glanced from face to face. But he was excited. 'I'm Tommy Jenner, this is my sister Marylou and these are my folks.'

Carmody rested his rifle against the wall. He signalled to his men outside, then turned back to face the room. He nodded for Old Shacker to take over.

'Ma'am,' Shacker said amiably, as though intuitively understanding who called the shots on the Cross H, 'we've come quite a ways. We're beat and hungry and came here looking for a quiet spot where we might rest our mounts some before we handle a job of work.' He smiled, eyes showing a winning glitter salvaged from his younger years. 'And I do believe we have found it.'

'You . . . you aiming to stay on?' Tommy asked.

' 'Course they ain't.' Ma sounded sure.

'I'm afraid your boy guessed right, Ma'am,' Shacker said.

'Over my dead body!' stormed Ma. 'By glory, you have a brass-bound nerve, busting in on honest folks without a by-your-leave and then announcing you plan on staying on. This is a free country amd we are honest, law-abiding citizens, and there's law hereabouts even if your kind mightn't care two hoots for it.'

'She talks too much, Wes,' growled Rip Creed, running his finger around the rim of fat in the skillet. 'Never could abide a gabby female nohow.'

'Let Shacker do the talking,' ordered Carmody.

As Shacker started up again, the Jenners continually glanced across at Carmody. He'd said little so far, but there was authority in his manner, something commanding about him. A body didn't have to be all that smart to guess who bossed this outfit.

Shacker spelled out their situation in an easy way. Their horses were worn out and men and animals needed rest and vittles, he explained. They didn't have much money but were prepared to pay a reasonable sum for board or lodging. They were peaceable and house-broken and would not cause any fuss.

When he finally wound up, Shacker glanced across at Carmody, who said:

'Any questions?'

'Yeah,' Pa said smartly. 'You boys toting any liquor by any chance?'

Creed laughed. 'Now, ain't that something? Here's a geezer who doesn't even know how long we might let him live, and all he's interested in is booze.'

'It's all he ever thinks of,' Ma complained. She drew a deep breath and stared at Carmody. 'But I have some questions . . . if I am permitted to speak in my own home, that is?'

Carmody nodded, and the woman felt the impact of his eyes.

'Just who and what are you? That's the first thing I want to know.'

Old Shacker promptly furnished five names they'd never heard of, then mentioned Carmody's surname, which they certainly had.

'Wes Carmody!' Tommy said wonderingly. 'Then . . . then you fellers are the Carmody gang?'

'Dead on target, sonny,' grinned Ben Yost. 'Dirt mean and loaded for bear – that's us.'

'So you're that wild man, Carmody?' Ma said wonderingly. 'My glory, you're not much older than our boy.'

'He's about the ringiest boy you're ever liable to come across, momma,' Jamie Yost chuckled.

'Keep a civil tongue in your head when you're talking with the ladyfolks, son,' Shacker reproved.

'Whatever you say, Daddy.'

'Don't pay these fellers no nevermind,' Shacker advised. 'They were reared rough and were never learned enough manners to carry grits to a bear, but you can be sure they'll watch their manners whilever we're your guests, ma'am. That's a solemn promise.'

'Please don't get mean with us, Shacker,' Ben Yost pleaded in mock fear. 'We promise to be good.'

'Hush your mouth, son,' brother Jamie said sternly. 'I swear every time you say a thing you bring down the family name. Where's your respect?'

'Right here,' Ben replied, and thumped his brother's shoulder with a hard fist.

'Son of a gun!' Jamie laughed, then whipped a headlock around the other's neck. They crashed to the floorboards then tumbled off the porch into the yard to roll away, punching and kicking like they were trying to kill one another.

Ma and Pa Jenner gazed on in bewilderment, but Tommy grinned, then began to laugh. Marylou returned and her mother could see she also was finding this violent display harmless and amusing, as it really was, underneath.

'This is not funny!' the woman snapped. 'Here! You two young animals, quit this instant!'

'Enough!'

Just one sharp word from the leader and the ruckus was over. It was then Carmody turned and saw the girl for the first time, and for a long moment seemed almost transfixed, so much so that finally the old outlaw cleared his throat.

'Only a purty gal, boy.' He then turned to Ma. 'What needs to be said, Ma'am, is that I'm afeared you might have us here for a spell. So I reckon the wisest thing for you folks to do would be . . . you know . . . just try and make the best of it.'

Pa Jenner rubbed his stubbled jaw. He was a runty little man with a whiskey-marked face and sparse hair capping a bony skull. Weakness had cut lines in his face and this weakness showed plainly when he spoke.

'Don't see no good reason why we can't offer these boys a little hospitality, do you, Ma?'

'You got no more sense than your children,' Ma retorted. 'We'll all likely get murdered in our beds tonight. And just look at the way that one is looking at your daughter.'

She jabbed an accusing finger at Demmon who was staring in open admiration at the girl. 'Keep your eyes to yourself, mister!'

'You can't rightly blame a man for looking, ma'am,' the gunman said. 'But looking is all he will do, you can take that as gospel from yours truly. Ain't that so, Wes?'

They waited for him to respond, but he was still staring at Marylou. Then he shook his head and swung to face the room.

'It sure is so. You have nothing to fear from us. But while we're here, I want it understood that none of you folks are to leave until we are gone. There'll be somebody on watch at all times, so I don't want anyone trying anything clever, such as tipping somebody off that the Carmody bunch is here.

'Tsk, tsk,' Ma clucked. 'Tell me, Mr Carmody, how does anyone as young as you get to be so cold and old?'

'It wasn't easy. Now, did everybody hear what I said?'

'Nothing wrong with my hearing,' Ma stated spiritedly. 'And now you've had your say, I'll have mine.'

'Make it short. We're all hungry.'

'Short it will be. All right, you can put up here, on account there's nothing we can do to stop you, but you'll pay your way and treat us with respect, hear? And I don't want none of you even so much as talking to my little girl here. Marylou has been brought up proper and I won't have her having any truck with the likes of you.'

'That all?' Carmody said.

'For the time being.'

'Good. Now I've got one last piece of advice for you, Ma Jenner.'

'And what might that be?'

Carmody jerked his thumb. 'Go tie up that mule. He's eating your greens.'

Vardino was there. . . .

Shad Fagan, the informant, knew it even before he turned in his saddle. He felt like a cold wind had just blown across his heart.

Yet there was no stirring of air in that silent badlands sunset. Fagan had come to the hide-out often enough to know exactly what it was that always warned of Vardino's presence.

It was the breath of evil.

The black crest of the Malpai Ridge had been innocent of life when Fagan looked moments before. Now, five lean riders on shaggy mustangs stood out against the skyline. Their faces were indistinct with the light behind them, but as they kicked their horses forward to ride down towards him, he caught the flash of Vardino's eyes like campfire light shimmering off a gun barrel.

He ran a finger around his collar. Damnit, wasn't he ever going to be able to get used to these people? Sure, the money they paid him for scouting and information might be good, but it was hardly worth it if he was always going to react to meeting them this way.

The Clansmen drew up around him in a semi-circle, the dust of the desert lands coating their clothes and savage faces.

Vardino spoke. It was always so. The marauder's lieutenants rarely said a word at such meetings between the spy and the leader of the ghost army that preyed upon the wastelands.

'You sent for me.' Vardino's voice was like the echo of a whisper coming back out of a cave.

Fagan swallowed hard, forced a grin. 'News from the nor'west, Asa.'

'Soldiers?'

'No, not this time. No . . . I reckon the last time the bluecoats come down here and got slit up by your boys they must've wised up they weren't going to get noplace so they likely—'

'If not them, who?'

The badlands spy swallowed, mean eyes darting from face to face again. These meetings were beginning to wear him ragged, never more so than tonight. Vardino acted like something was eating on his liver, and he was no easy companion at the best of times.

He coughed drily. 'Riders, pard. From the north. Americans by the looks of them. Six in a bunch travelling where scarce anybody goes these days. Lean, mean and packing plenty artillery. Sighted them last the day before yesterday crossing Dinnebito Wash. My hunch is they could just be bounty hunters looking to earn that big bounty the States has got on your head by this and—'

'That all?' the other cut in.

'Why, yeah, but . . . well, maybe it ain't much but. . . .'

'It's nothing! It could even be a story you dreamed up to squeeze gold from me.'

The words jarred Fagan to his bootstraps. There was something amiss here. He glanced quickly at the others, the chill in his guts turning to ice as he met bleak and savage stares.

Suddenly the badlands felt like the most dangerous place on earth, and he knew he must never, but never, come here again.

'Well . . . I can only say it's Gospel truth on account I seen them with my own eyes, Asa, but if the news ain't any good to you, well, hell, I ain't never been a greedy man. You don't have to pay me anything, I'll just mosey on my way and. . . . Hey, what are you doing, man?'

What Vardino was clearly doing, was slipping the long-barrelled revolver from the holster on his hip.

The first bullet struck Fagan like the Hammer of Thor. His hands clapped to his chest, he stared disbelievingly as the six-gun stormed, twice, three times. He felt himself falling as though from a great height. 'Why, Vardino, why. . . ?'

Had he said that, or was it only the murderous thunder of the shots that he heard which continued to pump into his scrawny body as he lay upon the uncaring earth of the badlands gulch?

The rugged Teofilo looked at his leader as he began to reload.

'Why, *Patron*?'

'He had outlived his usefulness.' The leader raised his gaze to meet his own. 'It can happen to any man at any time.'

Teofilo swallowed. 'Then you do not believe what he said about the gringos?'

'Perhaps.' The leader turned his prad with a jerk on the reins. 'Your task is to watch for these six . . . if they exist. I have much more to do. Do you have any more questions, curious one?'

Teofilo was a savage brute but with genuine courage. Yet he was grey beneath his olive complexion as he shook his head violently, telling himself the life of the Clansman, though rewarding, appeared to be growing more dangerous by the day. . . .

Satisfied his warning had struck home, Vardino jerked his horse's head hard about. 'Come, the way is long.'

They heeled away without a backward glance at the dead man. Spurring up the steep slope they rode with a skill that could only be matched by the only enemy they truly recognized and respected, the Comanches.

With the wind in his face, Vardino scoffed at Fagan's story about some lost pack of gringos sighted wandering across the fringes of the Rio Hondo

Badlands the previous day. Not even a dumb or drunken Americano could be that weary of life.

CHAPTER 4

CARMODY'S WAY

Wes Carmody, the man who never smiled, made his way slowly back down to the ranchyard from the hill where Ben Yost remained standing as look-out. With the ramshackle spread located on the outer fringes of the real badlands, eternal caution was essential at such times. Pa insisted the Clansmen never bothered them because – or so the old loafer insisted – the hellions knew there was nothing worth stealing on the Cross H.

Carmody appeared outwardly relaxed, an easy-striding figure in faded red shirt, hatless in the afternoon. He strolled across to the barn where Old Shacker sat in the sun upon an upturned crate, whittling white pine with a knife.

Wes hunkered down alongside him and they

talked quietly together so as not to disturb Jamie Yost and Demmon, both asleep within upon the hay.

Over by the corral, Rip Creed leaned indolently upon the slip-rails, trading stares with Juniper the mule. Neither man nor beast appeared impressed by what he saw. Creed had slept just a few hours coming towards morning. He was a restless man by nature, unsuited to inactivity.

Pa Jenner perched on the long pine bench that ran along the south wall of the house. He did a great deal of sitting. Sometimes he sat and thought, most times he simply sat. He was a self-pitying little loser who fretted about nobody but himself, who never ceased to complain of all the raw deals fate had handed Luther J. Jenner.

That day, Pa had more to occupy his mind than usual. The arrival of the outlaws was the most exciting event on Cross H Ranch since Ma received word of her legacy of the San Robles tract.

Soon, the family planned to up stakes and set off south, skirt the badlands, then cross into Mexico where Ma's brother had left his sister land in his will when he passed away from the colic in the spring.

They could have packed and gone had Pa been a little more willing and energetic; he liked the notion of moving to a bigger and better place, but feared it would mean more work than might be good for him. Pa had always yearned for riches that came easy. He admired men of style and natural authority. He even admired men who went out and stole whatever they wanted – men like Wes Carmody and his outlaw band.

Yet his passionate belief was that there was gold right here on the Cross H, if only he could find it.

His rheumy gaze switched back to the two outlaws hunkered down across the yard.

Carmody was a hard one to read, no mistake. Pa had rarely encountered a man who radiated so much strength and bitterness. Somewhere, he mused, somebody must have done that young fellow dirt and set a king-sized chip on his shoulder.

Whenever he got to thinking like this, Pa kept puzzling on something he'd once heard about a man named Carmody – something to do with Sheriff Reece Chandler down at Whiplock, he felt sure there was a connection, but realized he must have been too drunk to soak up all the details. . . .

A buzzard flew overhead, flapping southwards towards the Rio Hondo Badlands. Following the bird's flight, Pa's thoughts turned bleak again. Even a lousy turkey buzzard knew there was nothing worth stopping over for here on Cross H.

Smart bird.

The land was sour here and a man was hard put to run one steer to the acre. The cabin was old and falling apart, and if they packed up and sold out tomorrow they would be lucky to draw a couple hundred bucks.

He was watching Tommy nail up a loose fence slat when the sound of steps intruded on his thoughts. He turned his sorry head to see Creed approaching across the yard. The big outlaw scared Pa some, and his watery eyes focused on the big black gun riding the man's hip as he came up.

'What's the chance of a mug of joe?'

Pa rose stiffly. 'I'll go see, Mr Creed.'

'You do that.'

Pa hustled down the side of the house, the outlaw following more slowly. Ma and Marylou were in the kitchen fixing some chow. Ma was keeping her daughter close by today.

'Creed wants more coffee, Ma,' Pa said.

'Is that a fact,' Ma said tartly, but broke off when the gunman's head appeared in the window. 'Oh, very well!' she sighed, flouncing for the stove. 'Though how a body's expected to get any chores done with folks wanting coffee all the time, I surely don't know.'

Creed just grinned and leaned a muscular arm upon the sill. Pa went into the room and sat down, staring out at the big outlaw.

'When do you fellers figure on doing this job of work I've heard you talking about, Mr Creed?' he asked curiously.

'Dunno. I don't run this outfit.'

'Mebbe I should ask Wes?'

'Sure – ask the big boss,' Creed said, scowling

towards the barn.

'Must come hard, a man your age taking orders from a young feller like that?' Ma asked pointedly.

The gunman stared at her. 'Well, Shacker takes orders, and he's old enough for the discard deck.'

'But he's different from you.'

'Nicest thing anybody's said to me all day.'

'Wasn't meant to be,' Ma replied, ignoring her husband's warning look.

Creed grinned toughly. 'What's the game, mother? Trying to stir things up a little between us in the hope we might get to fighting, and that way you could get rid of us quicker, huh?'

Ma did not reply, but the way she flushed showed Creed he was on target. She did want them gone, even though they were proving no trouble. She simply wanted time and space in which to sit down and finalize her plans to pack up and leave for Mexico and their 'new life' there.

She poured coffee into a battered pannikin and passed it to her husband, who in turn handed it out to the outlaw.

'Much obliged,' Creed murmured, and walked away.

'Less said to that one the better, Ma,' cautioned Jenner.

'He doesn't scare me any,' Ma said stoutly. 'None of them does.'

'Scares me,' Pa said, scratching his belly.

'Everything scares you,' Ma countered, settling herself at the table to shell peas. 'Even the notion of travelling to Mexico for a new life.'

'We're not on that again, are we?' he complained.

'We are going this time, Pa,' said Marylou. 'This time for sure.'

'How's that again, girl?'

'We've been talking it over,' Ma said. 'This here business with the outlaws has just brought things to a head. I've decided we are packing and leaving just as soon as they've gone.'

Jenner had heard it all before. Ma had been unsettled ever since some distant kin had willed her a piece of cow country in north-eastern Mexico a spell back. This time though she sounded as if she really meant what she was saying.

'We ain't ready,' he protested weakly. 'Tommy's not proper growed yet, and you can't expect me to take on all the chores you'd find on a new place, not with my bad back, you can't.'

'We're going,' Ma reiterated, but in a softer tone now. She looked at him directly. 'We've got to go and you know that is so.'

'We ain't ready, I tell you. And even if we were, what about crossing the Hondo with the Clansmen out raiding like they been doing?'

'I've thought about all that, but it don't change my mind. We can travel by night and lie low during the day crossing the badlands. We can make it easy if we all pull together.'

He argued, but to no avail. Ma Jenner really had made up her mind. Jenner didn't know what scared him worse, the prospect of encountering Clansmen in the desert or all the work waiting at the end, should they make it.

He felt within him the stirring of rebellion and resolve. Why should he go? There was gold underneath his boots here someplace. Compare that with endless hard work or maybe a Clansman bullet in his back if he was to quit this quiet safe place for somewhere he didn't know and didn't want to. . . .

He was shaking by the time he finally quit arguing and mooched out into the yard. He just had to have a drink. Thank the good Lord for that jug of moonshine he kept planted in the back of the barn in case of emergencies.

Carmody and Shacker paid the rancher no mind as he slouched across the yard, and he glimpsed Creed prowling down by the creek. With a great show of nonchalance, Jenner rounded the corner of the barn in the dusk, then darted nimbly across to the pile of old hay. Dropping to one knee, he rummaged in the straw and came up with the gallon of moonshine he'd brewed himself in his home-made still before Ma put the axe through it. It had a kick like a mule, which was exactly what was needed right now.

The cork came out with an exhilarating pop. He

tipped the jug to his dry lips and drank deeply. He winced, waiting for the warmth to reach his belly. Then, sensing a presence, he jerked his head around to see Demmon leaning nonchalantly against the barn wall close by. The outlaw was smiling and looked thirsty.

'Sly old varmint,' Demmon drawled. 'Somehow I just knew you'd have a jug stashed someplace!'

Quick-moving and nervous, Marylou Jenner slipped from the house following supper while her mother was busy at the dishpan and hurried across the yard to the stables.

Ma had issued strict orders against her leaving the house tonight, and had even told her Rupert could fend for himself for just one night without being fed.

The girl always obeyed her mother, but her concern for the little calf was stronger tonight. Tommy had fed Rupert a bottle during the day, but she had to know the critter was well and warm or she would not sleep.

The night was chill with a wind blowing in off the Rio Hondo badlands. From her window, the girl could see the tall figure of Rip Creed pacing out the first leg of his nightwatch. Old Shacker and the Yosts were still at the house, drinking coffee and talking with Pa. She hoped Carmody and Demmon were at the barn.

The stables had had no door ever since Juniper kicked it down. The girl stood for a moment in the doorway, and stepped inside. The air was heavy with the smell of old hay and leather. She moved lightly between an old sawbuck and a horse collar to see Rupert's baldy face staring at her from the gloom.

Rupert sucked greedily on the bottle and she tweaked his ears as he drank. She wrinkled her nose at a sharp smell. She recognized it at once – Pa's moonshine.

She turned and saw a lean silhouette in the doorway. It was not the old man. Abe Demmon was drunk, yet had come in without a sound. The girl could see he was grinning, teeth white against the sunburned dark of his face.

Marylou moved fast, leaping to her feet. She made to dart past the man but a lean hand shot out and captured her wrist.

'Now, what's the big hurry, blue-eyes?' Demmon slurred. 'Seems this is a mighty fine chance for you and me to get acquainated.'

'Let me go!' she panted, trying to conceal how frightened she was.

He grinned, drawing her against his body. 'No chance, honeychild. My, but you are the softest little girl I ever did see.'

'No!' she cried, and clawed wildly at his face.

'Why, you little bitch!' he snarled, blood running down his cheek. 'Nobody does that to me!'

She tried to scream. He clapped a hand across her mouth, the other ripping at the bodice of her cotton dress. He was saying things that had no meaning and she was half swooning in terror. His strength, his rank gaminess and her fear . . . all were overpowering . . . and now she was being pushed to the floor with his full weight on top of her, smothering her.

A shadow fell through the moonlit doorway. The dark figure paused momentarily, then came forward. Demmon's hungry mouth was moving from the girl's throat to her breasts. Without warning an iron hand locked on to the back of his shirt collar and he was reefed upwards with such force that his breath was choked off. He twisted violently to catch one blurred glimpse of Carmody's taut face before a fist buried wrist-deep in his belly.

Demmon jack-knifed, retching with an ugly sound. Another vicious blow snapped his head back, the third smashed against the side of his face.

He went down in the straw and didn't even kick.

Still without a word, Carmody lifted his boot above the prone figure before the girl gasped, 'No . . . don't kill him. I'm all right – really.'

Carmody shrugged and lowered his boot. Smoothly he caught her up and lifted her to her feet. She tried to hold the bodice of her dress together, but without success. She was almost as frightened by his silence as she had been by the attack, yet she felt something else in her too, something strong yet not fully understood.

'Thank you,' she breathed. 'Thank you. . . .'

He was still silent, his eyes, so close to her own, holding an almost hypnotic intensity.

Then she felt his arm go round her waist. She trembled, yet didn't struggle. It was as though she couldn't, didn't even want to. His dark head bent close and she felt her hand slide round to the back of his neck, drawing him to her. Their lips met almost violently and she didn't understand any of it, and she was afraid and excited and bewildered all at the one time.

She didn't know how long the embrace lasted, would never know. Not for certain. Then above the drumming in her head and above the pounding of her heart, she heard her mother's voice:

'Carmody!'

They turned together. Ma Jenner stood four square in the doorway in her cheap print dress with meaty fists clenched at her sides. She shook with rage.

'It's not what it looks like. . . .' Carmody began, but broke off as Ma advanced like a two hundred pound embodiment of the wrath of God.

'And to think I thought you were the one gentleman amongst your pack!' she raged, and swung a punch that would have done justice to old Jem Mace himself, had it connected.

It didn't.

Ma Jenner could really hit, yet telegraphed her punches. Half-tempted to grin, the man who never grinned swayed easily out of reach of the haymaker, tightened his grip on Marylou's waist to sweep her off her feet then across to the moonlight spilling through the door.

By the time Ma had picked herself up, stumbled over a semi-conscious Demmon and struggled back out into the light, she'd used up some of her anger and most of her strength.

'Dirty—' she began, but her daughter, surprisingly strong and almost fully recovered by this, blocked her exit.

'Ma, you've got it all wrong,' she said. And while her mother stood snorting and gasping for breath, Marylou calmly explained what had occurred.

Ma was halfway towards believing her when Demmon came lurching out into the light, cursing and spitting blood. Vividly clear down the right side of his hawk face was the mark of raking fingernails.

Ma Jenner was never slow on the uptake. 'Why you filthy son of a—' she screamed, and only quick intervention by Carmody prevented her attacking the hardcase.

'I've dealt with him,' Carmody said sternly. 'He won't cause any more trouble.' He jabbed a finger at the outlaw. 'Tell her that's so!'

Demmon's pale eyes flared. He was a man of vanity, pride and lethal temper.

For a moment it appeared the two gunhands might grab Colts and settle things as their kind was prone to do. Yet finally Demmon faltered, dropped his eyes and backed up a step.

His words were barely audible. 'Sorry . . . damnit. It was the liquor on an empty gut and. . . .'

'That'll do it every time, pard,' Carmody said easily. He faced the women. 'You'll accept that, ladies?'

The girl flashed a ready smile, but her mother just shot Demmon a final scathing look then seized Marylou by the arm and made for the house.

'Damned old crow!' Demmon slurred. 'A man should—'

'Should do nothing and keep his mouth shut,' Carmody finished for him. 'I know you are a fool in drink, mister, but drunk or sober, you touch that girl again and you and I will come to it.'

Resentment flared in Demmon's sick eyes. 'Damnit, Carmody, you don't have to make a judge-and-jury case out of a thing. She's just a damned girl!'

Calm now, Carmody's look softened in the moonlight and his voice appeared to hold an unfamiliar gentleness as he moved off towards the house. 'Just a girl?' he murmured to himself in a wondering kind of tone. 'Mister, you are so wrong . . . she's everything. . . .'

And wondered what the hell he meant by that.

*

'Hurry up and wait!' growled Demmon. 'Tell me, how smart is that? We wear our horses down to their ankles getting this far, then someone decides we need to rest for – what the hell day is this? – Three days. Yeah, lay about getting into fights, horses all fit and rested up and so what does Carmody do then? Goes fence-fixing, is what. Tell me, old man, is that loco or what?'

Old Shacker drew his pipe from between his teeth. 'Wes might be a lot of things, but loco ain't one of them. He always has his reasons.'

'Or one reason,' Demmon said sourly, fingered the healing scratches on his face. 'It's the girl. Go on, old man, admit it.'

'You talk too much,' was all Old Shaker would say, and went mooching off leaving Demmon alone to watch what was happening over at the corral.

Carmody had pushed the tapered chock into the tight space between the railing and the corral post. He picked up the mallet and swung it twice, driving his wedge in tight. He tested the railing with both hands. Solid as a rock – now. Collecting two more chocks, he moved to the next post and repeated the procedure, with Juniper watching from a distance, darkly suspicious.

Up at the house, Ma Jenner poured hot coffee into a saucer and blew at it to cool it, her eyes never leaving the activity at the corral.

'Just what the tarnation does that man think he's about?' she asked rhetorically. 'His men want him to leave, yet he's busting himself catching up on all the chores you've neglected. You think the sun's tetched him?'

Shacker made his way across the yard and took his pipe from his mouth. 'Wes always liked to work with his hands.'

'Doing what? Shooting folks?'

'He's no killer. None of us is, for that matter.'

'You don't have to lie on my account.'

'It's so. We're outlaws on account they made us so, but we ain't killers.'

'Humph! What about them Clansmen the twins told us about you fellers shooting?'

'Clansmen don't count, lady. Leastways they don't in my book.'

Across at the corral Carmody was testing the rails again. The job was almost done. Ma Jenner hated to concede that his work appeared as though it might even withstand the famed hind-kicking talents of their ugly brute of a mule.

She said grudgingly, 'Where'd he learn to do work like that?'

'On his place up north.'

'He had a ranch?'

'Sure did. Fine little spread too. Had a ranch, money in the bank and a real fine life.'

'What happened?'

Shacker studied the bowl of his pipe. 'A sheriff he reckoned was a friend framed him for robbery and got him sent to prison. He broke jail and has been riding the owlhoot ever since.'

'A likely story.'

'Happens to be true.'

'Pshaw! Every thief, crook and swindler in the country sings the same song. Your friend – or boss or whatever he might be – is no better than any of his breed. And he'd better keep his crooked eyes off my little girl too if he knows what's good for him.'

At that moment Marylou appeared in the doorway. She wore her best dress and Ma had seen her double-brushing her hair earlier. She saw the way the girl gazed across at the corrals, and didn't like it one bit.

'Your chores finished, miss?'

The girl just nodded. She appeared lost in whatever she was looking at – and just the way she was looking caused long-suffering Ma Jenner to mutter several words rarely heard on the ranch.

She let another one fall from her mouth when she realized Carmody had finished up and was crossing the yard toting his tools under one arm. It galled the woman to realize she had never seen a more striking man, nor one who smiled less, if at all. It really rubbed in the salt when she realized his eyes were fixed on her little girl almost as though hypnotized. What in tarnation was going on here anyway?

'Well done, sonny!' a familiar voice croaked from behind, and Pa Jenner emerged from the galley clad in long johns and undershirt. He shook a fist at the distant mule. 'That will limit your mischief, you crop-thieving mongrel!' He broke into a big grin as Carmody mounted the steps.

'Hey, while I got your attention, son, your boys tell me you're off down into New Mexico after you finish up here, to tend to some business. If that's so, mebbe you'd be good enough to take Ma and the kids along with you on account they wanna leave, but I don't. What do you say?'

Carmody's thoughts were elsewhere. 'Huh?' he grunted, coming into the shade.

'Pay no attention to the man,' huffed Ma Jenner, turning for the door. 'He'll go when we go . . . he just likes to hear himself talk.'

Carmody shrugged and glanced at Marylou. Her eyes were the colour of bluebonnets, and he felt it again. The hit to the heart that he'd experienced the first moment they'd met, yet which he'd managed to ignore until he'd taken her in his arms while rescuing from Demmon.

He knew he was in love for the first time in his life. Yet how could something like that happen to a bitter man like himself when revenge was all he ever thought about?

'This place is gonna make me rich one day,' he dimly heard old man Jenner say. 'Sure wish you boys would stay on a spell and help me do some fossicking and maybe. . . .'

His voice trailed off when he realized everyone had disappeared inside where the cooking smells were coming from.

'I mean it,' he muttered, gazing out over a landscape as bleak as the backside of the moon. 'I ain't taking off to no Mexico . . . they'll be sorry when I strike it rich here . . . just wait and see. . . .'

Tommy looked eager. 'You fellers are getting ready to leave, ain't you?'

'What if we are, kid?' Creed responded, handling a heavy saddle one-handed like it was a feather.

'Can't I go with you?'

'What the hell would you want to do that for?' Old Shacker growled. 'Your whole clan's threatening to shift on to New Mex themselves any day now. They'll need you. Anyway, we don't take nobody with us nowhere, especially not on this here long ride, nosiree!'

For a moment the boy was diverted by intense curiosity. He'd sensed from day one the gun bunch to be *en route* to someplace on an important and likely a highly risk mission.

'I know you're making for Whiplock, old man,' he said. 'But what's for you there? You hiring out your guns, mebbe?'

'Man's business, sonny. In any case, like I say, you

got responsibilities right here.'

'They can take care of themselves. I want—' The boy broke off upon finding Carmody looming before him.

'What you want, kid,' Carmody said, 'is something more under that hat than hair. Your folks have looked after you all your life, they are planning on taking a big step to improve your life, and right when they need you to repay them some by helping them make it to where they want to go, you want to cut and run! Seems to me that with a mother and sister like you've got, you should be working your tail off to make life better for them, rather than looking to cut and run.'

Tommy's jaw sagged. Everyone else was staring at Carmody. They appeared puzzled, and were. It was unlike the leader to sound off over nothing much, which this situation appeared to be.

The moment passed. The kid went off with his face burning and Demmon and the twins returned their attention to their horses. Carmody stood isolated for a time, was turning to go when Old Shacker blocked his way.

'What?' he said, still testy.

'Don't take it out on the kid, Wes.'

'Huh?'

'Your bad conscience of course.'

'What bad conscience?'

Shacker's lazy gesture encompassed the unpainted

ranchhouse.

'Leaving these good folks to make their way across part of the badlands to get to where they're going – without proper protection. That's what's eating you today . . . has been ever since you fell over your feet for that pretty girl. . . .'

'You've got to be drunk, old man. You know the business I've got waiting in Whiplock can't wait any longer. . . .'

Carmody broke off. He could hear the anger in his own voice. More, he understood the reason for it. For there was a nagging sense of guilt at the thought of leaving Marylou behind, knowing as he did he had fallen in love for the first time in his entire life, but he had to admit an ugly truth: his hatred for the sheriff of Whiplock was even stronger. And this business would not wait.

He cleared his throat.

'Sorry, oldtimer . . . I'd do things different if I could, but I can't. You want to help me check out my cayuse?'

The older man studied him a moment, then nodded. Together they went down the steps and crossed to the barn where they were soon busy with the animals. While they were so engaged, Demmon entered leading his grulla and looking the worse for wear. Carmody shot the hard man a scowl, but then paused, gripped by unease and uncertainty. Driven by the hunger for revenge, was he growing too hard, he wondered? Surely the first real signs of this were already beginning to appear. . . .

He dropped what he was doing and walked across the barn where Demmon stood currying his prad.

'How you feeling, Abe?'

Demmon's surprised look slowly faded as he straightened. 'All right, I guess.'

'Er . . . you shouldn't drink, you know.'

'Sure I do.' Demmon thrust his Stetson back off his forehead with his forefinger. 'That little girl. I never hurt her, did I?'

'Not as much as I hurt you.' Carmody paused, examining a skinned knuckle. 'I didn't do any damage, did I, man?'

'Hell no,' Demmon grinned. 'We're tough *hombres*, remember?'

Carmody thrust out his hand. Abe Demmon gripped it hard.

'We'll make out fine down south, Abe. We'll do what we have to do then maybe cut on down into Old Mexico for some sinful living and high times. Right?'

'Sounds good, Wes. And while I'm feeling kind of shaky and not like my ornery self, I might as well say you're the best man I've struck to ride the river with.'

Carmody was moved, for Demmon was tougher than old bootheels. The warm feeling of camaraderie stayed with him and helped – without actually erasing – the secret guilt he felt for quitting this spread right when Marylou Jenner likely needed him most.

With a deliberate act of will he schooled such thinking from his mind. Nothing or nobody must prevent him reaching Whiplock now, and fast. It was as if he'd hammered that notion into his brain for so long nothing or nobody could divert him. Only revenge would a set him free.

CHAPTER 5

RIDE BACK TO REVENGE

He was ready for the trail.

Carmody stood in the chilly grey light of the false dawn in the ranchyard watching the gang saddle up for the long ride.

He'd shaved with cold water by lamplight in the barn and the skin of his face felt tightly stretched across the bones. Dark hair tumbled from beneath his hat across his brow. He wore a faded shirt and dark pants with the heavy gunrig buckled across his hips. He looked the complete outlaw, but for one thing.

The eyes.

On this chill New Mexico morning with the day

stretching uncertainly before him, Wes Carmody's grey eyes lacked the flinty intensity of a man setting off to settle an old and bitter score.

Disturbed by all the early activity, five Dominique hens had emerged from beneath the porch and scratched in the hard yellow sand. From the corral, battered yet still intact, Juniper the mule peered malevolently over the top railing. Pots clattered noisily in the lamplit kitchen. Ma Jenner was up and about, but had no intention of emerging to wave them off or wish them God speed, he knew. They couldn't be gone soon enough to suit her, now. Maybe now she might get to complete her own delayed plans to shake the dust of this accursed place off her shoes once and for all!

Rip Creed tightened up the cinches on his buckskin, adjusted the stirrup leathers, then dropped the saddle skirts. The buckskin gusted breath into the air as the husky outlaw drew his Winchester from its scabbard and worked the action. Satisfied, he replaced the weapon and glanced round at the others. The Yost twins had finally finished saddling and were now trading punches just to warm up in the chill. Demmon had already mounted while Old Shacker stood by his horse blowing breath into cupped hands.

Creed glanced across at Carmody and nodded. They were ready.

Yet still the leader made no move to mount. A

black cigar jutted from his teeth, but he hadn't lighted it yet. He stared across at the house as the light gradually strengthened. Juniper brayed derisively, a loud sound in the stillness.

The outlaws traded puzzled glances. What was he waiting for?

Suddenly she appeared at the front of the house, muffled in a dark shawl against the chill. They saw how her hair gleamed like gold as she moved forward to the edge of the porch. Her smile was tremulous as she raised her hand and waved to Carmody.

Carmody's right hand lifted slowly to touch his hat brim, his expression unreadable. Next instant he was in the saddle, heels thudding against the stallion's ribs. The big horse shot away, scattering the hens and sending the echoes of hoofbeats bouncing back off the barn.

He didn't look back. The cavalcade wound up the hill trail behind the house, men and horses dark against the strengthening yellow light. Briefly they were outlined in silhouette against the sky, then dropped from sight.

It grew very quiet again on Cross H Ranch.

The stagecoach wheeled into Main Street with its carriage swinging far over the thoroughbraces, the team were running fast and the coach sucked up a whirlwind of dust behind it.

Postmaster Jack French stepped out on to the

gallery of the Whiplock Post and Telegraph Office, shaking his head as he always did whenever Murphy Haines drove.

Any coach Haines brought in could be relied upon to be running late, due to that gabby driver's habit of halting to gossip with everybody he chanced to encounter along the way. Yet as soon as he neared a town, the man would whip up the team in order to bring it in headlong, flashy as a young cowboy despite the fact that he was well past fifty and as grey as a horned toad.

The driver delayed until almost abreast of the post office, where he swayed back on the lines and engaged the brake lever with a kick. The wheels locked and the rig slewed to a halt, throwing up an enormous billow of butter-coloured dust that started French coughing.

'Whiplock!' Haines bellowed unnecessarily for the benefit of his passengers. Then he seized the canvas sack from the rack in the back and tossed it down to French, who barely managed to catch it.

'US mail, Jack!' he bawled, just in case the postmaster might think he was delivering a forequarter of salted buffalo meat. Then with a laughing, 'Ho!' he lashed the teamers into action again and rumbled off for the depot.

'Some day,' French grumbled to his assistant as he walked back inside toting the sack, 'somebody's going to drag that big-nosed idjut down off of that high seat and boot him all the way out past the town limits for carrying on the way he does. Only hope I'm here to see it.'

'Mebbeso, Jack,' grinned young Lonnie Dellinger. 'But he sure breaks the monotony, don't he?'

French just grunted as he set about sorting the meagre supply of mail, yet privately conceded the boy might have something there. For Whiplock was a quieter place these days and the post office likely the quietest place in town.

French liked his work, but often thought back nostagically to the days before Sheriff Chandler took over, when drunken brawls or savage knife duels were prone to erupt at any tick of the clock day or night, and a full week rarely went by without seeing Jack Malleroy's hearse make its familiar journey up South Hill to the cemetery.

Chandler's iron fists and implacable adherence to the letter of the law had changed all that.

Monotonous now, he wondered? He supposed that was the price a man paid for law and order. Occasionally there might be a brief shoot-out or throat-slashing return to the town's old days of infamy. And those infrequent yet hair-raising brawls could always erupt and threaten to destroy the town. These outbreaks were invariably quelled by the marshal and calm was restored – until the next time.

The arrival of the mail coach always brought customers along to the office, but half an hour later things were just as quiet as before. Dellinger fooled with his telegraph key while the postmaster speculated on which of two flies on his blotter would be first to take off.

Suddenly both flies became airborne together as the door creaked open sharply and a stranger walked in.

The staff of the Whiplock Post and Telegraph viewed the newcomer with interest as he stood just inside, removing his kid riding gloves. He was tall and dark-headed in a faded red shirt and low-crowned black hat. His eyes were of a singular clear grey, black-lashed and penetrating. His gaze swept the office before he approached the counter.

'Yes, sir?' asked French.

'Any mail for me?'

'Name, sir?'

'Carmody.'

'Carmody. Well, I don't think so, but. . . .' French broke off suddenly. He blinked then went owl-eyed. 'You did say Carmody?'

'Wes Carmody.'

French swallowed drily and darted a glance at his assistant, who had turned pale. He cleared his throat. 'Guess there's no mail for anybody by that name, er . . . Mr Carmody.'

'Too bad. I applied for a skunk-hunter's licence. Asked for it to be mailed here.'

He nodded and left, tall in the doorway before he

disappeared. It was totally silent for perhaps ten seconds in the Whiplock Post and Telegraph Office, before Jack French suddenly found his voice.

'Lonnie, go fetch the sheriff. Fast!'

'Another cup of coffee, Reece?'

'Better pass, honey. Time I was back at the jailhouse.'

'It won't take a minute.'

'You're a temptress, Jane Chandler.'

'I've never denied it, have I? Come on, sit down. I won't have you pacing and fidgeting while you drink.'

Reece Chandler's reluctant sigh was as phoney as a three-dollar bill. For the truth was that of all the many things he liked doing, just lazing about the house talking with his wife was top of the list.

Dropping into his chair, the sheriff of Whiplock watched his wife move swiftly and lightly about their small, sunlit kitchen.

Jane Chandler was no great beauty, yet possessed greater charm and grace than any woman he'd ever known. His wife and his home were his refuge from a job that could swing from peaceful to murderous within the blink of an eye, and often did, although with less freqency now than had been the case in Whiplock's 'bad old days'.

He would never swap jobs with any man, for he was a lawman through and through. Yet it was always good to escape from the office during one of the quiet times. A man could easily grow hard and morose in his job without the benign influence of a wife and home life. Like Mr Briggs, who had never been so grim and dour as he was now when back in Hannibal, before his Emma passed on. Chandler wished his deputy might meet someone who would make him a little more human.

Jane fetched the coffee to the table and they sat discussing Chandler's recent patrol.

Sheriff and deputy had just returned from a two-day scout out along the Rio Hondo border to assess the current Clansmen situation. They had encountered no further encroachments beyond the Hondo, but had heard about an outbreak of killing and plundering farther south in the direction of the Rio Grande.

Just that morning Chandler had got a letter off to the Army at Fort Such suggesting they step up their patrols in the region, but didn't expect anything to come of it. The Army had its hands full with Victorio's Apaches who had broken out of the reservation again.

Prior to Chandler's appointment as sheriff of Whiplock this frontier town had been in poor shape. It was situated in the heart of the mediocre cattle country which stretched all the way out to the borders of the harsh desert lands and surrounded the county on three sides here.

Before Chandler introduced his rigid brand of law-enforcement the populace had been teetering on the brink of abandoning the town and leaving it to the Indians, the Clansmen and whatever other breeds of barbarians might threaten it.

The sheriff finished his coffee yet still lingered. The town seemed uncommonly quiet today. They had nobody in the cells and the wild cowhands wouldn't be in from the spreads until the week's end. As far as he was aware the only job he had on the blotter at the moment was the mysterious disappearance of Widow Hanlon's prize turkey. He felt that 'challenge' could likely wait.

Determined to take advantage of his unusually relaxed mood, Jane rose and went to the kitchen to fix more coffee. It was then that she glimpsed the familiar gaunt figure of Mr Briggs approaching the front gate. She sighed in resignation and was setting the pot aside when she realized the deputy appeared unusually grim, even by his sombre standards.

'Reece!' she called. 'It's Mr Briggs. I smell trouble.'

Chandler scooped up his hat and went through to the front porch with his wife following. He stood hands on hips as Briggs mounted the steps. The deputy was plainly agitated.

'What is it, Mr Briggs?' the sheriff asked sharply.

It took a moment for the deputy to catch his breath. 'Trouble, Sheriff . . . mebbe the worst kind.'

'Clansmen?'

Briggs shook his head. 'I said the worst, Sheriff. Wes Carmody is in town.'

Chandler went very still, not even moving when his wife clutched his arm.

'Carmody?' she gasped. 'You mean Carmody ... from Hannibal?'

'That's the party, ma'am,' Briggs affirmed. 'Your one time best pal. Walked into the post office all covered with trail dust and smelling of desert just ten minutes back. He ... he said something about expecting a skunk-hunter's licence to come by mail. . . .'

The lawman nodded slowly, grimly. For just a moment he'd allowed himself to hope Carmody's reappearance in his life after so long might not represent what he feared. Now he knew different. He knew who and what the 'skunk' was that Carmody had come hunting.

Himself.

He flexed wide shoulders as the shock slowly passed. He was calm and assured as he turned to his wife. 'Everything will be fine, honey. You're not to worry. I handled Wes before. I can do it again.'

Jane Chandler was white, but she knew what was expected of a lawman's wife. The calm in her voice matched his own as she replied, 'I know you can. But just be careful, won't you? For my sake.'

He bent and kissed her cheek.

'Aren't I always?' Then he fitted his hat to his head in a deliberate, unhurried way before turning away and going down the steps. 'Well, come along, Mr Briggs, we'll see what the man wants.'

Briggs paused on the porch, the big shotgun clutched in his gnarled hands. 'Nothing bad will happen to the sheriff, Mrs Chandler. Me and Beauty here will see to that.'

Jane nodded. She appreciated the deputy's attempt at reassurance, but it didn't really work. For in that moment before he turned to follow her husband's tall, upright figure down the path, Jane had seen that the deputy's hands upon the metal-scrolled butt of the shotgun were less than steady. She had never known Luther Briggs to show fear before, and she had seen him in several blood-curdling situations while backing up her husband on the streets. She could only assume the deputy was afraid of this man Carmody. How could that help but send a lance of cold steel through her own heart?

The lawmen did not speak as they walked shoulder to shoulder towards Main Street.

They had been together in wild Hannibal; had arrested Wes Carmody together; had both felt the intensity of the man's rage and hate at the trial when he'd accused them of a frame-up. He was like a man convinced of something in his heart and soul and would never stop believing it.

Each sensed that the hour ahead might prove

their greatest challenge since coming to Whiplock, at one time damned as the most dangerous town in the South-west.

Main Street appeared curiously deserted as they rounded the corner. Chandler raised a hand and they paused to watch several men hurrying along Elm Road in the direction of the Ace Corral up on the slope. Crossing the street at an angle, they looked along Elm to see a crowd surging about the corral.

The deputy grunted, 'Reckon he's up there all right, Sheriff.'

Chandler made no response. There was bitterness in him now as he glimpsed a man and a women emerge from a side alley, then head for the corral, jittery with excitement. The town plainly anticipated violence and nobody wanted to miss it. He could understand the scum reacting that way, but as they strode on he glimpsed solid, law-abiding folks whom he thought he'd come to know well – and who respected him – acting just as excitedly as though this were some kind of sport.

He glanced sideways at Briggs to catch him running his fingers over the scrolled base-plate of his shotgun. 'You won't be needing that, Mr Briggs,' he said evenly. 'I can handle this.'

'But what if you can't, Sheriff?'

'Then I have no right wearing this badge,' Chandler replied, and strode off ahead down the street.

After several paces he turned his head, expecting

to see the doughty deputy trailing him, despite orders, but of Briggs there was no sign.

This was astonishing enough to halt the lawman in his tracks, for Briggs had been the loyal shadow he'd been unable to shake off in their four years together.

He shrugged and began to climb again. He had something vastly more threatening than his deputy's behaviour to occupy him here today.

Elm Road was wide and dusty, running east to west. The Ace Corral had an open yard with several stalls extending across the alley. Directly opposite the Whiplock Cash Store stood J.B. Ruger's photograph gallery, and Vasey's Butcher Shop, it's façade still riddled with bullet holes from a murderous incident preceding the sheriff's takeover.

Already, upwards of a hundred people had assembled in front of the shops, yet for Reece Chandler the street might as well have been empty.

All the sheriff saw clearly was the tall figure standing alone against the inner fence of the corral smoking a cigar.

A sudden hush descended when Chandler strode into the yard alone. Twenty yards distant, Carmody stood with one arm resting on a rail, studying the glowing tip of the cigar in his hand as though it might hold the key to some great mystery.

Chandler saw immediately how greatly his former pard had changed. The lean physique that radiated so much power was the same, but the hawk face with its cold grey eyes was not that of the easy-going, laughing Wes Carmody he'd known in Hannibal.

He halted twenty feet distant, a formidable figure of authority in plain check shirt, leather vest – and gunbelt. 'Howdy, Wes.'

A stare as cold as sleet transfixed him. 'I owe you something, Chandler.'

The words, though soft, carried to the now hushed crowd. 'Still griping about Hannibal, Wes?'

'Still.'

'So?'

The lawman's one word was a challenge, raw and naked. And it seemed to the onlookers that in that moment – as they had witnessed before in times of trouble here – their peace officer appeared to undergo a visible change. Subtly, yet dramatically, Reece Chandler appeared to transform from a quietly spoken peace officer to a flinty fighting man – such a man who had countless times here confronted hellions and miners and drunken bums, not with the guns but with those iron fists clenched at his sides. Invincible fists.

Carmody nodded. He knew this man's ability with his hands, but was undaunted. In the year since they had faced, he had grown harder than he would have believed possible – and had never confronted a man he had not bested. 'So,' he said so all could hear, 'I always pay what I owe.'

There was a sudden scuffling of feet in the

background, a surging movement of onlookers moving back from the corral, from the facing men. They had come to witness something exciting here today, but were suddenly aware there could be such a thing as too much excitement should gunplay erupt, which suddenly appeared possible.

'Are you saying you've come here after all this time to try and kill me?' Chandler demanded stonily.

'That would make it quits for what you did to me, but I'm no killer, Chandler, never was. And I'd never have become an outlaw but for you and your stinking lies and what they did to me. But that's past. I can't undo what's done, but I can do what I've waited a long year for.'

'And what's that?'

Carmody deliberately unbuckled his gunbelt and hung it off a post. Then he removed his hat and placed it atop the gun before coming forward, hands on hips.

'I can give you the whipping of your life, Judas! I can deal with you in front of all those who hold you to be so fine! I will rub your face in the dirt of this town the way you rubbed my name in the filth of your lies in Hannibal.' His voice went up a notch. 'That's if you have the guts, of course?'

'Take him, Sheriff!' an onlooker shouted.

Chandler considered. He didn't have to accept this challenge. He could walk away – and be resigned to never hold his head up again in Whiplock. The town looked up to him as their two-fisted champion, the one man capable of protecting them no matter what the danger. They had come to expect it. If he failed to live up to their expectations he would be all through here.

But it was the other factor that saw him unbuckle his gunrig and fling it into the dust. For Carmody's eyes told him if it was not settled this way it would have to be done with the guns in a duel to the death.

The onlookers began scrambling for vantage points again as the two hatless figures began to circle in the corral dust. Although many were disappointed gunplay seemed to have been averted, they were excited by the prospect of a fist-fight between Sheriff Chandler and Wes Carmody which would surely prove to be something to tell their grandchildren about.

'This is foolishness, Wes,' Chandler said from behind cocked fists.

'Don't talk, man,' Carmody said, gliding close. 'You did all your talking in the Hannibal courthouse. Remember?'

He suddenly leapt with the speed of a striking catamount to crash a fist into the lawman's jaw.

'Ahh!' gasped the crowd as Chandler reeled from that tremendous blow. They expected him to go down, as did Carmody, but as Wes attacked again, Chandler found his balance and drove in a short right with the full weight of his body behind it. The blow caught his adversary high on the temple and knocked him down on one knee.

Carmody was back on his feet in a flash. The deep-throated roar of the crowd spilled over the rooftops and the almost deserted streets of Whiplock as two strong men came together in raging violence to resolve a bitterness that had simmered for one long year before exploding in flames.

What with all the shouting and hoo-rawing spilling downtown from Elm Road, and not a single customer in sight, banker Harley Middleton was having a hard time keeping his two-man staff gainfully employed.

'Murphy!' he snapped in his prissy, officious way. 'Have you completed the Barlow account?'

The teller dragged his eyes away from the front window. 'Er, not quite, sir.'

'Then get to it, and stay at it! And Stannard, I want the completed documentation on the Atkins mortgage on my desk before you leave these premises tonight. Understood?'

A fine state of affairs! The big-nosed little banker fretted, pacing to and fro between his tellers. Simply because some renegade from Sheriff Chandler's past shows up, the whole stupid town grinds to a halt!

Something caused him to swing and face the double doors. Did he hear foosteps? He did! Immediately greedy little eyes brightened behind wire-framed spectacles when he saw shadows through the frosted glass. Customers at last!

As the doors swung inwards, Middleton minced forward with a beaming smile, ready to demonstrate that no matter how many other so-called businessmen might be prepared to neglect their duties in town this afternoon, the management and staff of the Southwestern Deposit Bank most definitely were not.

The man propped in mid-stride, his welcoming smile freezing on his face as four strangers came trooping in.

And who could blame him?

Customers of the S.D. Bank never, but never, entered the premises toting six-shooters in their fists!

Middleton emitted one strangled squawk of alarm and terror before Rip Creed's gun muzzle pressed hard against his Adam's apple. The tellers sprang up from their desks, but were given no chance to reach their security guns before the wave of outlaws blocked them off. Murphy's hands shot up as Jamie Yost shoved a .45 in his face, but the gutsy Stannard took a wild swing at Demmon as the outlaw burst through the half-gate. Demmon's weapon cracked the side of his skull and he crashed to the floorboards.

'Not one peep out of anybody!' Old Shacker warned, brandishing his big Natchez Colt .44. 'All right, boys, truss 'em up and let's get to it.'

The outlaws worked with speed and efficiency to

bind the three men. Then Creed searched Middleton's pockets to locate the vault keys. He flipped them to Yost, who was singing, 'Easy, so easy,' as he darted for the vault.

Old Shacker moved to the windows to keep an eye upon the street as Yost unlocked the heavy studded doors and flung them wide. Creed and Demmon crowded behind him, peering in. The sight that greeted their eyes was a pauper's dream – wall-to-wall greenbacks.

It was but the work of minutes to fill the heavy canvas sack which Creed snatched down from a shelf. They could barely do up the drawstring when they were finally through packing it away. Their snap estimates ranged from five to fifteen thousand dollars. Middleton groaned impotently watching Jamie Yost execute a tap dance across the polished floor while pretending to eat a ten-dollar bill.

A sudden roar of voices floated down from distant Elm Road, the sound booming hollowly along the deserted main drag. One dirty chance in one million for outlaws to come riding in to find Main Street totally deserted – and they had come! Middleton thought self-pityingly. God must surely hate me!

Next moment he was jolted rigid by a sudden new thought.

Had it been simply chance? Or was everything – the brawl involving the sheriff and the whole moronic town rushing off to watch – actually some cleverly brazen criminal operation planned and timed down to the last split-second?

Was this how a great career in usurious banking was to end?

'*Adios, amigos,*' a smiling Creed called over his shoulders as they finally made for the doors. 'And just remember what all the smart ones say: money won't buy you happiness.'

They left casually, Creed leading the way out to stroll unhurriedly for the horses tied up in the flanking alley. A little old lady was tottering up the plankwalk when Old Shacker came out, weighed down by the bulging sack.

'Fetch and carry, fetch and carry,' he complained to the old woman. 'I do declare, some days it seems a body's work is just never done!'

Someone giggled and Yost clapped a hand over his mouth to stifle a yippee of triumph. They'd planned this down to the moment, and it had gone off without a hitch. 'So easy . . . so doggoned easy!' his twin brother beamed.

The little old lady leaned upon her cane and watched them swing into their saddles. She thought they looked wild and rough, and two or three plainly hadn't shaved today. Yet she concluded they must simply be young and happy to show such high spirits. What might it be like to be so young and innocent again?

'Right on time,' Creed remarked, gesturing

upwards at the town hall clock as they swung round the Holt Street corner.

The black hands of the clock showed four p.m. exactly. The solemn chimes tolling the hour rolled sonorously over the rooftops of Whiplock as they swung their horses on to the south trail and allowed them to break into a leisurely trot.

CHAPTER 6

PAYBACK TIME

The most welcome sound Wes Carmody had heard in a long while came with the distant chimes of the town hall clock from downtown.

At the end of fifteen minutes fierce fighting, Carmody's face showed little damage. His lightning reflexes and agility had prevented Chandler from landing a genuinely clean shot to the head up to then. But Carmody did have a shirtful of bruises as evidence of just how hard the lawman's body blows were, and by now his breath was rasping in his lungs like an ailing bellows.

Chandler was still on his feet, but only just.

The lawman's face resembled a slab of chewed beefsteak. Only sheer courage kept him upright. Chandler was the stronger of the two, but Carmody's dazzling speed, fuelled by the venom of a man with an old grudge to settle, had offset that advantage. The pattern of the brawl had been Chandler's relentless pursuit of his man, countered by the pistoning explosiveness of Carmody's counter-punching even as he back-pedalled.

But now Carmody was carrying the attack and the crowd began to quieten as they sensed him moving in for the kill. Three rips to the belly drew Chandler's fists down, and then the attack switched to the head. Blood flew and Carmody was cocking his right to deliver the finisher when a fist appeared to come from nowhere to crash against his exposed jaw.

He hit the ground on his back and rolled.

The crowd roared as Chandler lurched in for the kill. Spitting blood and dust, Carmody had to force himself to think back to what had happened in Hannibal in order to fire up his anger and thus give him the strength to get back on to his feet.

Chandler attacked, swinging, each punch meant to be the finisher.

But Carmody ducked, weaved and side-stepped his way round the ring of citizens until the fog cleared from his brain. He then propped unexpectedly and threw every ounce behind a right cross that speared between Chandler's cocked fists and exploded against his jaw.

He stood back and let the man fall. Chandler crashed face down with elbows briefly supporting head and torso off the ground. Then his arms gave way and his face hit the dust.

With chest heaving and the corral and the silent sea of faces swimming in his vision, Carmody turned and staggered across to the corner post for his gunbelt and hat. He found he was far too beat to even attempt to put them on. He spat blood into the dust, sucked in a ragged breath and headed unsteadily for the gateway.

One outsized miner, a friend of the sheriff's, stood in his path.

Carmody kept walking.

It appeared he would stride right on by the miner, yet as he drew level, he swung the heavy gunbelt in a wide arc with tremendous force and deliberately smashed his holster and revolver into the side of the miner's face with all his strength.

A cheekbone broke with an audible crack and the man crashed on to his back and didn't even kick; he was out to the world.

It was a brutal blow, the vengeful reaction of a man whose whole life had been ripped apart by lies, and delivered to the lawman responsible for false-swearing him into prison and eventually on to the outlaw trail.

'Accounts squared, you lying, Judas bastard!' he yelled thickly back at the unconscious lawman as he reeled away.

The mob watched as though mesmerized as he

made three futile attempts to mount his stallion before finally succeeding. Heels banged ribcage and he started off, swaying in the saddle with his gunbelt dangling from his hand and bouncing against the animal's flanks.

Wes Carmody was virtually defenceless as he rode off along Elm Road, yet not a man attempted to prevent him going.

None dared.

Waiting for Carmody to rejoin them out by remote Crow Gap Creek, the gang had plenty of time to count their haul. Seven thousand five hundred dollars! More money than they had seen all at once since they'd robbed the Wells Fargo stage outside Fort Worth six months ago.

Too damned bad they wouldn't be divvying it up!

The Yost twins predictably took to slugging it out on the high bluff above the creek to show just how good it felt to be in the money again, even if only temporarily. Tough Creed looked on with amused tolerance, but Old Shacker and Demmon were nervous and subdued, scanning their backtrail. These two were not about to start any celebrations until Wes showed.

Excitement erupted twenty minutes later when the distant rider appeared. A short time later Carmody approached, safe and anything but sound, judging by his looks.

Ben Yost gave his brother a final kick on his shins then jumped astride his horse and raced out to meet Carmody and be the first to deliver the news of the success of the bank robbery.

They hardly expected Carmody to begin yipping and waving his hat. And he didn't. Nonethless, he appeared satisfied if a little seedy when he rode up and swung down along the bulging leather satchel with the bank insignia emblazoned upon its flanks.

'Good work, boys,' he said simply as he began stripping off his shirt.

'Hey, Wes,' Jamie Yost called, 'ain't bath night already, is it?'

'Close enough,' Carmod panted, discarding pants and boots before heading for the water. He hurled his aching body into the creek headlong, took a long and deliberate time surfacing, then rolled on to his back and floated, blowing a siphon of water into the air,

He remained totally submerged again for fully a minute, allowing the healing water to soak into his aching body like a benediction. It was only when he emerged and walked back towards them that they saw the full extent of his savage bruising.

'Great day in the morning, son!' Old Shacker exclaimed. 'Did that dirty lawdog take a mallet to you?'

'He was even tougher than I figured,' he grunted, pacing to and fro to dry off.

'Did you whip him, Wes?' asked Ben Yost.

'I whipped him good.'

'Did you leave him alive?'

'Yeah.'

'Should've shot the bastard for what he done to you,' Demmon said toughly. Then he blinked and said, 'Just exactly what did the lawdog do to you that fired you up the way it did, Wes? I mean, all we know is he done you wrong way back when, but seems we never got round to hearing the story. . . .'

Carmody began climbing into his pants, aware of a ring of questioning eyes. For it was true. They knew he carried a huge grudge against Sheriff Reece Chandler, knew Chandler had somehow done him wrong in the past, and that revenge against the man had been his driving force both in prison and since. They further knew that they would not keep the money stolen in today's successful robbery, a condition all five had had to agree upon before coming to Whiplock. But surely, in the flush of success, they should now be allowed to understand why?

Wes sat on the brickwork of the old ghost town's choked-up well.

'I did what I set out to do . . . what I'd been planning for a long time,' he told them, eyes turning distant. 'You see, Chandler and I were buddies in Hannibal back then, him sheriffing, me horse-breaking and riding gun guard on the gold coaches.

One night, Chandler was out of town and he left Deputy Briggs and me to guard a gold shipment that came in too late to go to the bank.

He paused to shrug.

'I'd handled stuff like that for him before – we were buddies and trusted one another. . . .' His face hardened. 'That night the gold went missing. Briggs claimed he'd dropped off, but I was awake and I heard or saw nothing before Chandler came back at dawn and found the shipment missing. I was the only one who could have stolen it. Leastways that's what he and the deputy claimed. It was a lot of money. The County Commissioner ordered I stand trial, they found me guilty and I wound up with you bunch of losers in prison . . . end of story.'

They digested the tale in silence. Then Old Shacker spoke up.

'So. . . ?'

'So, he ruined my life and I wasn't going to sit back and take it,' he said harshly, getting to his feet. 'I figured it out behind bars. Chandler ruled Hannibal and Whiplock the same way . . . with his fists, with raw guts, grinding the hellers underfoot. The iron lawman afraid of nothing. That's why the honest folk love him. He tamed their town in Whiplock and everybody looked up to him. So, in one day I brought him down. I showed he could be whipped . . . and while I was whipping him somebody busted the bank he was supposed to protect above all town banks, meaning the town is ruined.'

He paused and spread his hands.

'He's finished . . . and we're square at last. Any questions?'

They stared at him admiringly. They were men who understood revenge, who liked to see high-steppers cut down to size. Each had admired the iron Carmody since the day the John Laws escorted him to the prison, and in return for their loyalty he'd taken them with him when he escaped.

They owed him plenty, but were paying a big price for their loyalty today. . . .

'Now Chandler's reputation is wrecked for keeps,' he concluded. 'If he doesn't get fired after today then Marshal Moran isn't the stiff-necked old sonuva I reckon him.'

He paused, buckling up his pants. He was looking back, savoring his success. It had taken a long time to plan and finally execute his get-square against the man who had robbed him of his good name and had him jailed.

'The whole scheme went like clockwork and it feels damned good,' he half-smiled, his tongue probing at a loose tooth. He looked at them sharply. 'Any questions?'

Looks were exhanged, heads nodded, easy smiles appeared. During their time riding the high lonesome with Carmody the gang had waited to learn the real story behind his imprisonment and eventual escape. Now they felt they could fully share an innocent man's commitment to revenge.

'Well, son,' Old Shacker said, firing up a Bull Durham cigarette, 'now that's behind us, nothing but fine weather and easy trails ahead down to mañana land, huh?'

Buckling up his gunbelt, Carmody said, 'Well, just about, old timer, just about. . . .'

'How's that?' Creed asked sharply.

Carmody fingered damp hair back from his forehead and replaced his hat. 'First things first. Fetch me the sack.'

A silence fell as Creed crossed the yard to heft the heavy canvas sack with the words WHIPLOCK BANKING COMPANY stamped upon it in bold letters. He returned it to Wes who slung it over one shoulder then crossed to the ancient, weed-choked well in one of the tumbledown ghoster's back yards.

They followed curiously.

What was he fixing to do?

It didn't take long to find out.

Wes kissed the leather satchel then reached out and deliberately dropped it into the well where it was instantly engulfed by a tangle of choking grasses and vines.

They gathered to stare down. There was nothing to suggest a fortune in cash and gold lay secluded here. Nothing about the ghoster to indicate anyone had visited here in a coon's age, which was exactly as it was intended to look. Wes straightened.

'I'll let the town know where they can find the money only when Chandler has been sacked and shamed and kicked out,' Wes stated. 'Not before. If they haven't already fired him by a certain time I'll let them know what they will stand to gain if they do so. It wasn't enough for me to whip the bastard. I'll have him busted down to nothing or Whiplock will never see their money again.'

Nobody responded. They'd always looked up to him but today's achievements had illustrated more clearly than anything before just what Carmody was made of. Reaffirmed in the most convincing way that the longer they remained loyal to him the greater their prospects of survival, maybe even ultimate freedom and prosperity? Who could tell?

Such were their feelings in that high moment, but they were tough, independent and volatile men by nature, as was about to be proven. . . .

Calmly Wes rolled and lit a brown paper quirley. He inhaled deeply. He felt good.

'OK,' he announced, pacing to and fro. He took a deep breath. What he was about to announce might not prove too popular. 'More good news, boys – I hope. We'll be heading for Mexico – by way of the Cross H Ranch.'

Creed instantly started in cussing.

'That ragged-ass outfit is miles out of our way. Why the tarnal do you want to go back there for? And what in hell do we want in Mexico?'

'Figure we owe the folks something,' Wes replied coolly. 'The thing is, they need help to make it south and I aim to see they get it.'

'That's the most crack-brained thing I ever heard of,' Creed exploded. 'What'd they do for us except what they had to? That fat old lady hates our guts. She would likely take a scatter gun to us if we was to show our faces back there again now.'

'We'll take a vote,' Carmody said calmly.

'The hell we will! Every time we vote in this man's army everybody goes your way.'

'That's what they call democracy, Rip,' grinned Shacker, trying to make light of it. 'Anyways, I don't see it as such a bad notion. Real fine woman that Ma Jenner, even if she tends to be a bit sharpish at times.'

'They sure treated us hospitable, Rip,' Demmon weighed in. 'And if Wes thinks we should help—'

'The hell with that!' Creed snarled, swarthy cheeks taut with anger. He shook his head violently. 'No, by Judas, those crackers ain't getting no help from me!'

'Then that makes it your choice to quit,' Carmody said quietly.

'Hey, easy, man,' said Demmon. 'We stuck by you to pull that big caper back in Whiplock, but we didn't agree to running a Clansmen gauntlet across the Rio Hondos . . . just because you're hot for that little lady back there.'

'It's that bit of skirt, ain't it, Carmody?' Creed

accused, encouraged by Demmon's support. 'You fell for her – I seen that plain as day. And because of that, you're looking to us to risk our asses just so's she will know what a big man you are. You're asking far too much, man.'

A weighty silence fell. Carmody folded his arms and studied the gunfighter calmly for a long moment before replying.

'I told you beforehand how we would do it, Creed. You agreed. Sure, any man is free to change his mind. Only thing, no man who doesn't go with the vote doesn't get to ride with me.'

The tension deepened. A split had never seemed so close before.

'Don't push it, Rip,' Old Shacker advised. 'We've been through too much together to break up just when we're riding high on a big victory, pard.'

'Wes's big victory, you mean,' Creed said angrily. 'We were just the stooges playing our part—'

Before Creed could respond, Jamie Yost shouted down from the bluff. 'Hey, Wes! Riders a-coming!'

They rushed up the slope, Carmody leading the way. As they approached the crest, they glimpsed the long line of horsemen strung out along the horizon in the far distance. Wes swore softly. Looked like he'd underestimated that hard-knuckle town!

'Posse!' Ben Yost gasped. 'Didn't take them long to get organized, did it?'

'How many do you make, Wes?' asked Shacker.

Carmody watched the horsemen round a sweeping bend in the trail then come pounding on. 'Fifteen to twenty,' he hazarded. 'Big bunch . . . so it's time to make tracks.'

He swung to confront Creed. 'No time for any more jawing now, Rip. So, how's it to be?'

Rip Creed ground his teeth. He was angry enough to make the big break, but not so angry that he couldn't see the future: back to riding alone again, most likely. No high times, no hair-raising excitement like they'd all shared just today. He resented Carmody because the others held him so high, but did he hate him enough to want to go return to the High Lonesome, every hardcase's worst dream?

'All goddamn right,' he said thickly. 'We'll do like you say. Crackers clans . . . Mexico . . . the goddamn badlands . . . Clansmen thick as flies on a pot roast! What the hell! We'll tackle them all if the great Carmody says, but I'm warning you fair, Wes, you will—'

'Tell me the rest in Mexico,' Carmody interrupted, then led the way to the horses at a run.

CHAPTER 7

SOUTH BY RIO HONDO

Chandler raised a hand to bring the posse to a halt. They had reached a fork in the trail where still-fresh tracks branched off south-east. The lawman frowned, then winced at the discomfort this simple movement brought to his battered face.

With hoof-lifted dust swirling about them, he sat staring out along the twisted trail that wound away into the scrubby hills ahead of them.

'What's the delay, Sheriff?' demanded banker Middleton. Looking ridiculous on horseback, the man would be saddle-calloused within the next ten miles, but had insisted on joining the posse. If the outlaws were not captured and the stolen funds retrieved then little Harley Middleton – and half the businessmen of Whiplock – would surely be ruined.

'We won't be delayed for long, Mr Middleton,' Chandler replied.

'I should certainly hope not!'

The sheriff inhaled cautiously, massaging his ribs. Doc Muster had called him a blamed fool for taking on a manhunt in his condition. But sick and sore though he might be, Chandler would see it through to the bitter end, even if the pursuit led all the way to Panama. He was made that way.

'What do you think, Mr Briggs?' he said to the deputy.

The same Doc Muster who'd treated the sheriff had extracted two of the deputy's broken front teeth and slapped a strip of plaster over his nose before the posse set out. Briggs might not look chipper, yet the sheriff had as much confidence in the hardy deputy's ability to stay the course as he had in his own.

'They must mean to hole up someplace in the Rio Hondos, sheriff,' Briggs opined, sounding like a man suffering a bad head cold.

Chandler put a deep stare on the man. There had been harsh words between the lawmen in the wake of the disaster in town. Understandably, it would appear, the sheriff had wanted to know howcome Briggs had seemingly vanished at the very hour he was fighting the battle of his life against Carmody – while the outlaws calmly and coolly plundered the bank.

Howcome the most loyal and reliable of deputies had disappeared at the day and hour the sheriff had needed him most?

But, reminding himself time was rushing by like a maniac with a knife, Chandler hipped around in his saddle and glanced back over his hastily assembled posse. 'These men will find it hard going if that proves the case,' he speculated. A mixed assortment of cowboys, store-clerks and soft-handed townsmen did not comprise an ideal posse.

'It'll be tough for all of us, Sheriff.'

'Most likely, most likely.' Chandler threw his right arm forward. 'All right, let's ride!'

They followed the difficult, winding trail with Chandler riding well ahead, reading sign. The six sets of tracks showed clearly enough in the dust. Six sets of tracks, and five men had held up the Southwestern Deposit bank. . . .

Five thieves and one Carmody tallied six.

The thought caused Chandler to compress battered lips.

Wes Carmody had planned and executed his revenge brilliantly, he was forced to concede. The man had known he would fall for his challenge to fight rather than settle their differences with the Colts. Carmody had suckered him into that brawl like he was a simple tinhorn. Naturally the fight had attracted half the town, and while Carmody was playing cat-and-mouse with him at the Ace Corral his gang had calmly ridden into a semi-deserted town and cleaned out the bank without a shot being fired.

Simple as child's play!

And he'd let himself be suckered into it like some green hick!

Reece Chandler had never been so convincingly outsmarted and humiliated before. In his own defence he firmly believed that, a year ago, he'd have emerged the winner, but he'd been beaten, not by the Carmody of Hannibal, but this new steel-tempered Carmody one brutal year older and fired up on revenge.

He believed Carmody would have beaten him today even if he'd had to kill himself doing it.

Then the thought came again. Why did Carmody hate him so when all he had done back in Hannibal was his simple duty as a lawman?

Back then, a shipment of cash had come in unexpectedly at night and he'd been obliged to house it at his jailhouse. When an emergency arose he'd left the shipment in the care of Carmody, his rugged friend, and Briggs, the trusted deputy. When the money vanished it was plain stolid and reliable Deputy Briggs' long and spotless record was his best defence.

Therefore Carmody's guilt was seen as complete and overwhelming. So, what was he trying to prove now?

He shook the thoughts away angrily. Time for soul-searching later. Much later – when he had Carmody in chains and the bank loot secure in his saddle bags.

He stared down at the empty spot on his shirtfront where his star had been worn.

He still found it hard to believe. The marshal of Milltown had shown up in town mere hours after the fight and robbery to conduct an investigation. By the time he'd heard about Chandler's 'unprofessional' brawl, he'd been deeply affronted and when it became obvious that the sheriff had been suckered into that fight in order to make simple the execution of the robbery of the bank, all that was left was to impose the penalty:

'Dismissed for unprofessional conduct – with a relief sheriff to be sworn in as quickly as possible.

Case dismissed!'

He bit his lips. His shadow stretched long upon the land. It was approaching sundown. He gigged his horse into a faster lope. He tried not to think too much about the Rio Hondo Badlands by night. Or the Clansmen.

A tumbleweed rolled drunkenly across the Cross H ranchyard before coming to rest against the south wall of the house. Chickens squawked disconsolately from the barn. The corral gate hung open, creaking in the wind.

'I tell you I don't like this, Wes,' Demmon protested, six-gun in hand. 'That fat old lady could be lying for us.'

'Two women, an old man and a kid got you scared, Abe?' Shacker taunted. 'You sure are a two-fisted fighting hellion, aren't you?'

'Hello the house!' Carmody hollered for a second time.

No response.

The tumbleweed started off again, rolling on by the deserted corral and finally finding escape through a section of broken fence which Pa Jenner never had found the time to fix.

'I'm going in,' Carmody decided. 'Cover me just in case.'

Rifles and six-guns were raised as he heeled the stallion across the empty yard. The sun was gone and dusk was deepening across the flats and creeping up the flanks of the scrubby hills. Carmody reined in a short distance from the house. He called once more without drawing response, then swung to the ground.

Colt firmly in hand, he bounded up on to the back porch. He paused, listening. Not a sound. Nothing. A quick glance through a window revealed the kitchen to be empty. Two swift steps carried him to the door. He kicked it open and went on through in a low crouch.

'Marylou!'

His voice echoed hollowly. The room appeared bare with the pictures gone from the walls, cupboard doors hung open. He went quickly down the hallway, peering into the gloomy little rooms.

The Cross H ranch house was as empty as a last year's bird's nest.

He was retracing his steps for the kitchen when a shot crashed from the yard, followed by shouting. Bursting out on to the porch, he glimpsed Creed lifting his Colt .45 to trigger towards the old barn again.

'Somebody in the barn, Wes!' Shacker shouted, his words swallowed by Creed's next shot.

A wild cry sounded from beyond the barn doorway. 'Don't kill me! I'm coming out!'

They stared as little Pa Jenner crept out of hiding, trembling like a tumbleweed in an August wind.

'Jenner!' Carmody snapped. 'What's happened here? Where are the others?'

'Gone, Mr Carmody.'

'Gone?'

'Long gone. Can I let my hands down now?'

'Drop them and talk fast,' Carmody rapped as the others closed in to join them. 'So, where's the family?'

The little man gestured southwards. 'Took off to Mexico. Ma bundled everybody up and headed off in that bull-headed way she's got, took Marylou and Tommy and all she could tote in the wagon with that cussed Juniper in the shafts. She'd been threatening to quit and take up that there tract her folks left her for almost a year, but I never reckoned she'd do it, but she is sure gone . . . leaving poor old Pa to fend for himself the best way he could.'

'They're not crossing the Rio Hondos?' Old Shacker gulped in dismay. 'In high summer . . . raiding time?'

Pa nodded. 'Yeah, says she planned on travelling mostly by night and sticking mainly to Cracker Canyon. Like I say, always was a hard-headed woman, my wife. I tried to talk her out of it but she never did pay me no mind.' He paused to scratch the back of his neck. 'Of course, she was fretting some about the daughter and—'

'Marylou!' Carmody said sharply. 'Is she all right?'

'Oh, sure. But she was acting kind of moody . . . might have had something to do with you, young fella. . . .'

Carmody swore softly, his expression grim. 'We know the Clansmen have been raiding again, maybe wider than ever this summer and remember, we saw smoke far out that last night that might have been. . . .' He broke off, shaking his head as he stared southwards. 'Mexico . . . goddamn. . . !'

'Mebbe she'll make it. Always was a mighty determined female that wife of mine,' Pa announced with the ghost of a smile. 'But I bested her this time round when I told her straight out I was staying put to find my gold vein. Yessir, I shore showed her this time.'

'You chicken-livered old son of a bitch!' Shacker snarled. 'You let that good woman and your kids go off into that hell country, knowing what might happen. A man ought to—'

'Easy,' Carmody said. 'You know, they say that mostly the Clansmen don't bother too much with this poor end of the Rio Hondo, but I guess we can't bet money that they won't. . . .'

'She'd have to take the long way round on account of that wagon,' the other speculated soberly. 'My guess is she'd likely travel south by Antelope Pass then swing back south to ford the river either at Mission or Carrizo. You figure it that way?'

Carmody nodded. They were familiar with the entire region, having drifted down into Old Mexico to elude the Texas Rangers soon after the jailbreak and, knowing the territory, they well understood its dangers.

'Wes!' Demmon called from his saddle. 'Look yonder!'

Turning, Carmody and Shacker saw distant dust drifting across the low hills they'd crossed some two hours back on their way in: hoof-lifted dust. The posse which they had glimpsed at great distance the previous day was plainly making ground.

'Let's hustle!' Creed said urgently.

Carmody and Shacker traded looks. Each knew what the other was thinking. With a posse on their heels they needed to travel both far and fast – not waste time reading trail sign or staging a search that could be like looking for a needle in a haystack.

He forced himself to put it all calmly into perspective before he made any more decisions.

He'd figured from the outset that Chandler would never quit on him. Therefore, the only thing on his mind right now should be flight. Should be, maybe, but it wasn't. Nothing like it. . . .

'We'll take the badlands,' he said, and felt proud when not a man objected this time.

Apart from Pop, that was. 'What about me?' he bleated as they swung up, but all Pa's chickens had come home to roost, and the outlaws' contempt showed plainly as they stormed away, shrouding him in their dust.

'Why me? Why is it always me?'

He was still standing there in the darkening yard, shivering with self-pity when the posse vanished over the far rise, hoofbeats swiftly stuttering away into silence.

The desert night's chill was seeping into Tommy Jenner's bones as he lay sprawled behind the stand of cactus above the dry creek bed. But he wouldn't move, he dared not.

Cold metallic moonlight flooded the landscape of badlands, it appeared as cruel and alien-looking to the boy's eyes as the far side of the moon. Far out across those windy wastes, barely visible in the ghostly moonlight, he thought he could see a slow-moving line of riders.

Clansmen? he asked himself.

He blinked and realized his overwrought imagination was playing tricks again. He really could not see a damn thing out there except the wild and unforgiving badlands, seemingly frozen under that bloated moon. Yet overwrought instincts told him that far, far out there, they would be playing their flutes to make that hauntingly eerie music familiar to all who challenged this brutal land. It often proved to be the last sound they ever heard in this life.

Sweat coursed down his cheek and he brushed it aside.

Another quarter-hour passed before his imagination finally shook off phantom riders and the ghostly music of Clansmen flutes.

He waited and watched for some time further before rising to scuttle back down to the wagon.

The dry bed of Cracker Canyon where they had made camp wound its way far back into humped and broken hills to lose itself finally in the shadows of the giant buttes. This was a dry and lonesome land, haunted by the coyote and the wolf, and often in summer by human predators. It was a no-man's land of sand and heat through which a nameless watercourse threaded its way.

'Tommy?'

Ma's call sounded from beyond the bend ahead.

He could tell just by the tone of her voice that she had spoken with the rifle butt pressed to her cheek. She was ready to start blasting should anyone but her son come creeping up through the dead grass.

The boy grinned admiringly. Ma was just as tough and full of sass out here in the middle of nowhere as if she was standing flipping the bacon atop her pot-bellied stove back home.

'It's me, Ma. They've gone.'

Ma Jenner lowered the rifle as her son emerged from the gloom. He tugged off his hat and grinned reassuringly at Marylou who held a heavy, rusted old-fashioned Colt in one slender hand.

'It's all right, Sis,' he assured. 'They were too busy tootling their goddamned flutes to pick up on our tracks.'

'Tommy!' reproved Ma. 'Language.'

The boy grinned and Ma went over to check Juniper's headstall. The mule glowered malevolently at the woman as she leaned back against the wagon shaft to gaze up at the rim-top. She reached into a pocket of her voluminous jacket, took out the map and consulted it by the light of the moon. It had proven reliable thus far and she was confident it would get them through. They had passed Cottonmouth Arroyo at midnight; it was some ten more miles to the Puma Hills and Antelope Pass.

The pass would be their halfway mark. There would be no point in turning back from there for whatever reason. Such had been Ma's thinking before their first distant glimpse of the terrifying riders. Now she was suddenly and uncharacteristically unsure just what they should do.

Trudging back to rejoin the children, she decided to put the matter to the vote. It had been her impulsive decision to set out on the long-delayed journey, yet with danger threatening she felt all should have their say on whether to continue onwards for the Valley of the Rio Grande or head back to Cross H.

Marylou and Tommy were both scared, having for the first time finally experienced the chilling impact of journeying across what the old-timers of the regions simply referred to as 'out there'. The Rio Hondo was a forbidding and haunted place and yet both insisted they would rather press on than return to the poverty and hopelessness of Cross H.

Ma embraced them both and dabbed at her eyes before returning to the wagon.

'All right, you miserable, loafing wretch,' she snapped at the drowsing mule. 'Time to get back to work!'

The animal looked murderous as the passengers climbed back atop the load. When Ma hollered 'Giddap!' he dropped his ugly head and refused to move one inch. He was staying put.

Dust flew from mulehide as Ma applied the whip. 'Hup, you miserable fleabag! Hup!'

The ugly brute stood its ground until Ma struck a match and held it close enough to his burr-laced tail to singe the bristling hairs a little. It grunted, twitched its ears, and they were off at a good clip.

'Should make the hills by sun-up,' Ma predicted as they cleared the creekbed and rolled south-west. 'Then we'll rest up and hide all day, move on again come dark-down.'

Perched upon the high plank seat on her either side, Tommy and Marylou nodded in silence. They watched the landscape owl-eyed as the moon slid low in the clouds. The terrain appeared lifeless and truly alien now. Clouds formed in the high purple skies then drifted west on the gentle breeze. All remained superficially serene as they slogged their way onwards, yet the sensation of watching eyes and lurking presences remained and even seemed to grow stronger than before.

Marylou closed her eyes and pictured the man she loved whom she knew she would never get to see again. Her mother saw a tear roll down her cheek and promptly took her feelings out on the mule with a sharp slap of the leather. This brought no violent reaction this time. For the sinister atmosphere of this country by night had grown so oppressive it was even succeeding in scaring the meanest critter in all the wastelands.

CHAPTER 8

BADLANDS AND BADMEN

Old Shacker had risen in the dark of early mornings to milk cows every day for fifteen years from the age of nine. Old habits remain strong and he automatically awoke before first light every day of his life. A gibbous moon hung low over the torn and broken country. He raised himself on one elbow and stared dumbly out at the brush, only gradually recalling where he was.

He grinned toughly and flung the brightly colored Fort Lincoln blanket aside and got to his feet.

He realized this was the first morning he'd woken up rich in far too long. Or should that be 'technically rich?' he idly wondered. Should they survive this hell country by some miracle, and make it back to the north some day to retrieve their cache, it would only be to return it to the Whiplock Bank – the way Carmody had planned the whole operation from the outset.

He supposed it had been a a pretty crafty plan of revenge, when you considered it. First whip the 'unbeatable' two-fisted sheriff before the whole town to destroy his invincible reputation. Then, while Chandler was busy brawling like a drunken miner, have 'bandits' clean out the bank and so bring the town to ruin.

If a lawman didn't get fired for that level of dereliction of duty, then what would it take?

Chandler's humiliation and dismissal would at least prove a partial revenge for Wes, he supposed. Too bad there seemed no way of clearing his name of the original crime – the disappearance of that bank shipment which Carmody had guarded and had 'lost' two years earlier.

Dressing quickly, he gazed up at the gnarled limbs of an ancient tree that coiled and twisted against the dim stars, then smiled again. He'd always found the stars of the southlands brighter than anyplace else and wondered if this might prove an omen of further good luck.

The eastern breeze rose, as it often did, with the coming of dawn. An invisible finger of wind stirred the brush and dusted powdery alkali over the sleeping figures of Creed, Demmon and the Yosts huddled close by.

Beating his arms against his chest to warm up, Shacker moved off for the broken butte which reared gaunt and high on the north side above their camp. The band had settled here some three hours earlier after crossing the gnarled and broken badlands from the Jenner place. Horses and men had finally demanded rest. Somewhere backtrail, he figured the posse would be resting as well. Maybe. . . .

The long grey streak in the eastern sky was taking on a crimson flush by the time he'd clambered up to Carmody's ledge. The two stood watching the slow coming of day in silence. Carmody had a blanket draped over his shoulders and sucked on a dead cigar. Studying him, Shacker couldn't guess what he was thinking, but then he rarely could.

'Sight anything while I was asleep, Wes?'

'Dust and smoke,' came the response. 'Dust was blowing north-west about two hours back, more was showing to the south-east just afore you came up. And see, you can still see traces of something in the sky to the east.'

The wind toyed with Shacker's grey hair as he peered east. He could barely make out the smoke in the sky, but could pick out a little dust haze to the south.

This eerie feeling he experienced reminded the old-timer of Kansas during the big redskin wars before the War Between The States, when a man could be feeling chipper until he looked out to see smoke and dust on the skyline and knew painted redskins were abroad and raiding.

Yet the menace out here did not come with red feathers and painted headdresses, but rather in dust-grey coats and hats along with repeating rifles.

The camp was stirring below.

Down there, Creed was dimly visible moving amongst the horses, while Abe Demmon torched his first cigarette of the day into life. The sound of the scraping match awakened Ben Yost, who sat up disgruntled. He immediately tossed a boot at his sleeping brother's head. His aim was good, considering he'd just opened his eyes. There was a thud of contact, a curse, a flying blanket, and Ben Yost was sent crashing over on to his back by one hundred and eighty pounds of enraged brother on the hoof.

'You'd reckon that pair would act a little more dignified by now, wouldn't you, Wes?'

'Why now?'

'Well, on account they're technically wealthy men, not saddle bums.'

'Oh yeah . . . I keep forgetting. . . .'

Shacker studied him sharply. 'Forgetting all that folding green we stole . . . and are honour bound to return to that crummy bank. You must have something burdensome on your mind to forget something like that.'

Carmody did not reply. His narrowed gaze was focused upon the north back in the direction of Huley Gulch. With light spreading more swiftly across the sky now he was able to make out a faint patina of rising dust.

He snapped his fingers and pointed. 'Chandler's in the saddle. Time to travel.'

The sun cleared the rimrock as the party rode out. Wes rode with his eyes not on the south in the direction they were travelling, nor back northwards where the possemen's horses were kicking dust into the sky, instead his gaze focused east where the broken-backed ridges of the Puma Hills chopped the skyline.

And there it was! More thin dust rising gently, and plenty of it. Could be upwards of a dozen horsemen on the move out there . . . maybe horsemen who called the wastelands home. . . .

'Beats all,' Old Shacker murmured after a silence.

'What?' Carmody grunted.

The old outlaw gestured. 'More dinero than we ever dreamed of; that hardnosed sheriff left licking his wounds way back in our dust; a fine sunny day coming on and yet you look like we were riding to a funeral or something.'

'Maybe we are.'

'Huh? Whose?'

'Yours if you don't shut up.'

Shacker just nodded, but didn't respond. He'd found out what he'd wanted to know. His trail partner was tense, indicating he was fretting far more about that girl today than yesterday. And squinting north at what they all reckoned to be Clansmen-raised dust, he supposed he couldn't rightly blame him.

Waiting for his scouts to return after the river crossing, Kruger, the Clansman chieftain, stared out over the brush-stippled desert floor that sloped away into the dunes. In unending succession the dunes undulated, rank upon rank against the deep blue sky, cresting like waves in a sea of sand as smoothly voluptuous to the eye as a sleeping woman . . . naked of course. . . .

The leader shook his head clear of pleasant visions and took out his cigars, thin black cylinders crammed with a tobacco fierce enough to cause double vision should a man inhale too vigorously.

As he moved, his leg brushed against bulging satchels and saddlebags. He smiled wolfishly, black eyes twinkling in the shadow of his sombrero. Although he hadn't had a woman since quitting the *Llano Estacado* two months earlier, his raiding parties had proven highly successful. There was loot aplenty and they'd seen enough killing to satisfy even the most bloodthirsty of his feral pack.

Now Mexico lay ahead, calling with all the

romance and mystery of his dark-eyed and honey-breasted south. . . .

The first scouts to return had nothing to report, but the three-man squad which came in thirty minutes later, did. The party had ridden westwards to sight rising dust near Yellow Feather Creek, sufficient to indicate a number of horses.

Kruger stroked his jaw. That many horses could suggest rich plunder, yet might just as easily indicate danger should they belong to lawmen or the army.

The last patrol came in a short time later from the north. They'd sighted nobody, but had cut sign. It was the fresh tracks left by an overladen mule-drawn wagon near Antelope Pass.

Kruger shrugged. One wagon? Scarce worth the trouble. How many in the wagon, he wanted to know.

'Three people, *caudillo,*' supplied the cadaverous killer with one ear missing. 'We see where they stop to fix the harness. One *hombre,* two *señoras.*'

Sudden interest flickered in the depths of Kruger's dark eyes.

'*Señoras?*'

'*Sí.* One old and fat, the other very young with small foot.'

'Near Antelope Pass, you say?'

'*Sí.*'

A slow smile crossed the leader's scarred features, and that old familiar hunger stirred in his guts. It was a long way back to the Stronghold and the arms of his Indian women. . . .

Abruptly the smile became a laugh which his henchmen understood only too well, and the hungry glitter in the leader's eyes was reflected in other faces as he bawled the order to use their spurs.

They rode northwest and an eager Kruger set the distinctive notch of Antelope Pass between his horse's ears.

Ben Yost was in one of his moods.

'What are we doing?' he asked, appropos of nothing.

'What's it look like? We're riding and sweating is what.' His brother wasn't in the mood for talk.

'I mean . . . what are we doing out here, you dumb son of a bitch. Riding the goddamned wastelands . . . risking our fool necks every mile. Why ain't we in Ringo City chasing skirts like we was planning on doing after Wes cleaned out that tinpot bank?'

'Because we're looking to save these folk, of course, you horse's ass!'

'We're not chasing that cracker family, stupid. We're looking to find the gal Wes is loco about. One dame. She's nothing to us, yet suddenly we're expected to run ourselves ragged and maybe get killed for her . . . instead of living high on the hog in some bordello in Bordertown. Don't that strike you as strange?'

Jamie Yost considered. He finally shook his head.

'No, it don't. And the boys don't think so either. You're the only one who does, which proves what I always claimed. You're an idiot!'

They wrangled for the next mile then sulked for the ten after that. But Ben Yost knew when he was licked. And when he came to reflect on it calmly, he supposed it felt good to be helping Wes out after all he'd done for them. Well, almost good, maybe.

The coffee was bitter and black, which was just how Chandler wanted it. He stood with a tin pannikin in one hand and a cigarette in the other, his back to the small fire they had lit at the bandits' overnight campsite. Sheriff Chandler had set out from Whiplock in the worst physical shape of the whole bunch, yet was now plainly the strongest.

Men moved sluggishly around him, dragging on cigarettes, stiff from fatigue and suffering with blisters. The hot emotions that had carried them from Whiplock with such energy had long since dissipated. They were making no gains on their quarry while the Rio was drawing ever-closer. There were those who would have quit long before this, had it been possible. But five miles back, when Jackson, the blacksmith, had announced he was quitting, the sheriff had rammed a six-gun in his belly. At that point both Jackson and everyone else understood it was far safer to continue on than attempt to quit.

Briggs approached Chandler toting the coffee pot.

The sheriff studied the man as he silently refilled his mug. Briggs met his gaze levelly.

'Something on your mind, Sheriff?'

'Nothing new, Mr Briggs. This whole affair just keeps raising that old question again and again in my mind. Why would Carmody still insist he was framed about what happened back in Hannibal? I'm talking about the night you and him had a shipment of gold vanish from under your noses. He said at the time he was innocent as a jaybird, and I saw plainly, back in Whiplock, that he still believes that.'

Briggs rubbed the plaster covering his busted nose. 'Visit any lock-up and nine men out of ten inmates will tell you they were framed.'

'But they're not men like Carmody.'

'What makes him different?'

'The way he was . . . the way he maybe still is. He always struck me as a man too straight to lie.'

'Sheriff, that night you left Carmody and me to guard the money shipment when the bank couldn't handle it, I had to go find you to sign those security papers, when I got back the shipment was missing from the back room. No sign of nobody, no explanation from Carmody – just denial that he knew anything. It was loco, it was stupid, but he was the only one who could have stolen that money. You figured it that way as did the judge, and nothing's changed since. Carmody stole that cash shipment and will be held guilty until the day he dies. End of story.'

Briggs sounded convincing. Yet Chandler wondered why the man was for ever either glancing away or dropping his eyes whenever the topic of the stolen money in Hannibal was raised.

'Then what does he stand to gain by claiming innocence over a year down the track?' persisted Chandler. 'He's listed as a fugitive in Texas, Colorado and Kansas and now New Mexico. What can he hope to gain by singing that old song?'

'I've never pretended to know how any outlaw thinks,' Briggs continued, 'but right about now I figure Carmody counts himself as good as safe, getting this close to Mexico.'

The lawman tipped the dregs of his coffee on to the sand. He nodded. 'He's got every right to feel that way, Mr Briggs,' he said quietly so nobody else would overhear. 'The truth of it is, we have very little chance of catching them before the Rio now.'

'Are you saying we will stop there, Sheriff?'

'We'll see when the time comes.' Chandler shook his head. 'We've been unlucky. If we'd pressed on a few more miles on our patrol earlier on in the week we might have stopped off at the Cross H and quite likely nabbed them there.'

'Yeah . . . and more'n likely got killed for our trouble.'

'You reckon so?'

'That's kind of a dumb question, ain't it? That bunch was holed up there in strength planning to hit the bank. They'd have cut us to pieces.'

'Funny thing is,' the sheriff answered, 'I was going over the records just the other night and there's no record of the Carmody gang killing anybody.'

'Dumb luck, I guess.'

'You could be right. Well, we're not making any headway standing here. Have the men saddle up.'

Chandler watched his deputy thoughtfully as he moved about the camp, barking gruff orders. He'd also observed that Briggs seemed irritable and strangely defensive whenever they discussed Carmody. He realized this had always been the case whenever Hannibal and the Carmody case came up. He had no notion why this should be so, yet it caused a strange feeling of unease, maybe even raised a dim shadow of doubt in the back of his mind. . . .

The feeling had left him by the time his horse was underneath him and he was riding out past the sentinel butte where the outlaws had posted their look-outs in the early morning hours. He told himself Carmody might trumpet his 'innocence' concerning the robbery of the Hannibal Express Office till his dying day, yet the law would continue to deem him as guilty as any man could be. Forever.

Carmody would pay the full penalty due eventually, he reaffirmed, and he realized that, without being aware of it, he had reached the decision to pursue his quarry beyond the Rio Grande and into Mexico if he must.

*

Tommy Jenner jacked a shell into the rifle chamber and waited. All around the rocky depression where he crouched, he could see them now – flitting grey shapes of the Clansmen darting from boulder to rock pile to tortured old tree trunks. . . . They slowly drew closer, always closer.

Ma suddenly opened up with that old Navy Colt and he saw the slug strike fire from a boulder, causing a menacing grey figure to duck low.

'Better go easy on the ammunition until they get closer, Ma,' he advised. His voice was uneven. Blood seeped through his shirt at the shoulder from the flesh wound he'd taken when the grey figures had first jumped them; it seemed like an eternity ago now. The wound hurt, but the boy could still use a rifle, could still fight on.

'Would you like a drink, Tommy?' Marylou asked, crawling up from behind clutching a canteen.

He nodded, set down the rifle and drank sparingly. It was mid-afternoon and the sun seared the wastelands; all the Rio Hondo area seemed to be on fire, but it was hottest of all down in their hell-hole saucer of sand and stone at the bottom of the basin with gunsmoke clouding the sky overhead.

'Hey, *amigo*!' a mocking voice called. 'What for do you shoot at us frien'ly fellows? All we want is to say 'ello to the lovely *señorita*!'

'Surrender!' called a stronger voice. 'You'll just make it harder on yourselves this way, vermin!'

'Scum!' Ma yelled back, and drew a stutter of bullets in reply.

Behind the defenders and lashed to the wagon, Juniper, the mule, pricked his ears up at the whine of flying lead then snorted with what could only be defiance.

Ma Jenner stared glumly across at the animal, then at her children. All so brave, she thought with a loud sniff. Of course she believed that mule would hate her with its final breath, but she took comfort from the fact that neither of her offspring had even hinted they might hold her responsible for leading them into this life-and-death situation.

Ma had vowed that they would never take her daughter alive. She had two slugs in the side pocket of her rough canvas jacket; they would be held in reserve for Marylou and herself.

The enemy began calling to them again, insulting, mocking voices spiked with cruel laughter. This was all merely a game to them, a game played out under a badlands sun.

The half-hour that followed seemed to take forever to pass with the enemy slinking ever closer and the defenders using their weapons only when a target presented itself. In that time one enemy was severely wounded and Ma's cheek was lacerated by a flying rock chip. Juniper sustained a bullet crease across the hindquarters, which appeared to only make him more defiant.

Then it came.

The lean, wolf-like shapes of three of the enemy broke cover and rushed towards the defenders' position with hair-raising screams and cries.

Ma and Tommy triggered together and a buckling figure nose-dived into the ground. Another reeled sideways, clutching at his shoulder, but the third kept coming, screaming like a banshee.

As Tommy feverishly worked the action of his rifle, Ma drilled two deliberate shots at the weaving figure without scoring a hit. The attacker leapt the final protective ring of stones with a blood-curdling scream and charged directly at Tommy just as his finger was tightening on the trigger of his long-barrelled Mexican five-shot.

Tommy jerked up his weapon and fired at point-blank range. The Clansman's momentum carried him forward to crash heavily atop the prone boy. Tommy's head banged against a stone and he lashed out blindly. For a moment, the attacker's eyes blazed into Tommy's with insane hatred, then began to glaze over.

Tommy shoved violently and the body rolled deeper into the saucer, dead with a gaping hole in his chest. They had survived. But for how much longer?

CHAPTER 9

KILLING GROUND

In the early afternoon Rip Creed's buckskin picked up a stone in the hoof and they were forced to stop. Creed got down, fumbling for his knife. Old Shacker sat in his saddle, bent a little now by fatigue, his jaws working on his chewing tobacco. Carmody also remained mounted at Shacker's side, his eyes playing restlessly over the alien landscape.

The delay was untimely. They were twenty miles out from their overnight camp, yet still a long ride from the red bluffs that marked the Rio Grande. The heat was beating off hills and naked plains, distorting the skyline. It was hot enough to make a lizard sweat and Creed's soaked shirt clung to his body.

From his high perch in his saddle, Abe Demmon drawled, 'Cuss a little, Rip, I hear it helps.'

Creed shot the man a venomous look then continued with his chore. The pebble was deeply embedded in the frog. He had to go carefully in order to prise it free without damaging the hoof. The wastelands were no place to have a horse go lame underneath you.

The dust smudge on the horizon behind was no closer than before, yet no further off either. Studying it, Jamie Yost lifted his hat and scratched his fiery thatch, a big patch of sweat showing under his arm.

'If there's one thing I can't abide,' he drawled, 'it's a goldurned ex-lawdog who can't take a licking like a man.'

'And if there's one thing I can't abide,' his brother growled, 'it's a man beating his gums for no good purpose.'

Jamie glared at his husky twin. He would dearly have liked to hand him a smack across the head for that, but it was too hot. It was almost too hot for anything.

At length Creed straightened, holding up a tiny pebble between thumb and forefinger. 'Got it,' he grunted. 'Let's go.'

'Hold a minute,' Shacker said, foraging in his possibles bag. He produced a small phial of liniment. 'Rub some of this in so's it won't get sore.'

Creed caught the bottle when he tossed it to him. 'We got time for this?'

'We've got time,' Carmody affirmed. Then he

stiffened, turning to face east. A small sound had disturbed the afternoon hush, a sound like distant summer thunder, but, as he listened intently, playing his gaze more to the north-east in the direction of the broken hills, he realized it was not thunder after all, but the low mutter of gunfire.

Nobody spoke for a few minutes. There had been no talk of the Jenners during the journey south, though the family had been constantly in the thoughts of at least two of their number. All were aware that the wagon trail south led through Puma Hills and Antelope Pass. . . .

'Hey, Wes!' Ben Yost hollered from behind. 'Where the hell are you going, man?'

No response.

It was just a moment since Carmody's keen hearing had picked up that first distant sound of gunfire coming from the west, the direction in which they were trailing the Jenners, and he had leapt to an instant conclusion.

It could be them! They might be in trouble!

Next moment, with spurs raking horsehide, he was thundering away just as fast as a good horse could gallop.

He was heedless of the confusion he left in his wake . . . he neither knew nor cared that the following minute Old Shacker had precipitately taken off after him.

Before the old-timer was gone from sight, the Yosts

followed too. They'd paused only a moment, shaking their curly heads in perplexity and then galloped off – such was the blind faith they put in the man who'd released them from prison and kept them both free and alive ever since.

Carmody calculated he'd covered some five fast miles, with the sounds of shooting growing louder by the minute before he topped the rim of a deep, sandy basin and reined in to stare down into a smoke-wreathed defensive saucer ringed by rocks a quarter-mile below. He could hear a deafening roar of guns and see mounted figures circling the besieged sector, returning the defenders' fire.

Clansmen! And surely he recognized that battered old wagon within the circle?

Carmody didn't hesitate, he dug in his spurs and, tucking his head in low upon the animal's neck, swept down the rocky slope at a headlong gallop. He triggered his six-gun and a howling attacker flung up his arms and tumbled from his saddle.

The defenders were at first incredulous, then amazed, and finally gripped by a kind of hysterical relief, when they recognized who it was. They realized his arrival – although plainly some kind of miracle – must surely mean they were saved and that doubtless his gang would show up in his wake.

Carmody did not believe in miracles.

And yet, upon witnessing – just a few gun-blasting moments later – the full-tilt arrival of Old Shacker and Jamie Yost, his disbelief in divine intervention took a hammering. They blasted way right into the inner, defensive circle after brother Ben was cut down by the howling enemy leader.

In the meantime, he gave it all he had, shooting raiders at Marylou's side.

For more than an hour the battle raged on insanely with the formidable support of what was left of the gang blasting their way through the perimeter and each bringing down his own share of attackers.

Carmody became aware that the longer it lasted the more slender their prospects were becoming. Sure, the apron area beyond their rock circle was now littered with dead and dying vermin, but the roar of the battle was drawing enemy horsemen from other quarters until it seemed the entire Clansmen brigade must now be assembled here in the basin, howling and hungry for victory.

Eventually they were totally encircled by a ring of deadly steel with belly-wriggling figures making their snake-like way in under the cover of supporting fire. And all the while a lone flautist played his eerie music from the ridges, inspiring them on. . . .

The next quarter-hour passed swiftly with the danger creeping even closer, the defenders now firing only when a sure target presented itself.

An exhausted Carmody finally lowered his overheated weapons and allowed Marylou to swab the sweat out of his eyes. The brutal exchange of gunfire seemed to be lessening, yet he knew this could only be temporary, for the Clansmen were still very close at hand. Soon the signal must sound for the final charge, and then their lives would only last a few seconds.

Deliberately he reloaded his Colts, stole one last look at Marylou and, incredibly, saw her smile bravely. Then he turned to await the final gun-down.

CHAPTER 10

UNTIL DEATH

The final rush came without warning as slinking grey shapes suddenly sprang up on all sides, darting from boulder to boulder behind crashing guns, no longer singing death songs but screaming their hate, emotion and blood lust lending them a courage their breed could rarely muster.

Hunched behind their feeble brush and stone barricades, the sounds of shooting and screaming were deafening to hear. Carmody's first awareness of something odd occurring behind the smoke-shrouded attackers, was a glimpse of a horseman wearing a sombrero.

He blinked and knuckled his eyes for a moment before he saw an enemy suddenly turn to one side to blast at somebody behind him before buckling and crashing on to his back never to move again.

'What the hell. . . ?' Carmody panted. Next moment he went rigid with disbelief when, through a gap in the enemy ranks caused by several of their number going down under scything gunfire from behind, he saw them coming in.

Gun-toting Americans with sombreros astride big, grain-fed north country horses were mowing down howling grey shapes before them like corn in a field. And most incredible of all, Carmody recognized the stalwart figure of the horseman leading the charge.

It was the ex-sheriff of Whiplock, Reece Chandler!

Carmody was quick to recover from his shock. He blinked and saw that the murderous gun battle raging before them in the open basin now appeared to be favoring the Americanos – but who could be sure?

He issued no orders, simply led by example. Delaying only long enough to reload both six-shooters, Carmody leapt over the feeble barricades and blasted a couple of shots that cut down two of the howling enemy, then plunged to the ground as angry lead came whistling back in response.

He felt a surge of pride when he turned his head to see Jamie Yost, Shacker, Creed coming after him . . . he was still tallying when Creed stopped the one that mattered most and pitched forward, reflexes working his .45 trigger for the last time.

Madness reigned as Carmody jumped up and recklessly spurted ahead through whistling lead to help the momentarily besieged Chandler. For a moment, the two previously close friends, who'd become such bitter foes, stared at one another. There were no words, yet something powerful passed between them, something unidentifiable.

Then a bullet howled close and together the two men turned to carve a bloody pathway through an enemy which was suddenly no longer attacking, but rather was faltering and howling in impotent rage and terror as their dead piled higher about them.

From the corner of his eye, and almost blinded by stinging gunsmoke now, Carmody realized there was an enemy segment running against the tide, a braver and more ruthless unit which was still pressing forward even as their beaten henchmen died or attempted to flee.

The party was led by a tall Clansman with shoulder length hair and a face distinguished by its ugliness and a demonic hate.

Kruger!

The eyes of the Clansmen's leader and the two gringos met and locked for an instant. Then all three triggered together, the American outlaw bobbed low at the vital second and kept his head bare inches beneath a howling slug. Carmody and Chandler fired together at close range and the killers' captain clapped both hands to his brow where their lead had gone. He tumbled dead from his saddle and one of his boots caught in the stirrup, causing him to be dragged away at the gallop, his body bouncing violently over rocks and brush and the bodies of the slain.

The vermin beyond were whipped even before Kruger had died, they just didn't realize it until he'd fallen. Yet even though shattered by this murderous attack from their rear, which combined with the stepping-up of fire still coming from the saucer's defensive line, they continued to make a fight of it until their vaunted former leader was sighted being dragged bouncing and bloodied through the dust behind a crazed horse like so much slaughterhouse trash.

They froze and stared wildly around through the sifting veils of dust and gunsmoke, coming to realize just how few of them were left . . . the entire basin floor was littered with the corpses of their dead.

They broke and ran.

None now moved to stop them. Victor and vanquished alike had had their fill of blood and death on a day that would mark the end of the Clansmen's long reign in the badlands, and had also brought two enemies and former friends together, face to face. . . .

It was some hours later that Marylou asked, 'What are they doing now?' Her voice was tremulous with uncertainty as she stood before the row of squat adobe huts comprising the township of Crescento which stood one mile from the big river and three from the corpse-littered battleground.

Ma snorted, 'Talking. You know what men are like. Well, they'd better get it over with fast if that Chandler feller wants to see that sidekick deputy of his afore he croaks. I just took a look at that feller.' She snapped her fingers. 'Close as that to Glory! And would you believe he told me he not only wants to see Chandler badly, but him and your fancy man both!'

'Ma, Wes is not my . . .' the girl began, then broke off. There was too much happening to speak, even to think clearly. As well, she was still so overwhelmingly relieved by the outcome of the fierce showdown, murderous though it had been, to feel much of anything but grateful just then.

She was curious, though, as she turned to look across at the adobe. What could they be talking about for so long in there? Her fear was, that such was the anger and emotion between them that Wes and that former sheriff might try to kill one another now they had finally come face to face. Impulsively she moved across to the stoop to listen by the partly opened door. After some moments she realized it was the former sheriff of Whiplock who held the floor.

'You don't expect me to believe that cock and bull story, do you, Carmody? You say you stashed that bank robbery money someplace near Whiplock to be recovered and handed back to the bank after I was fired? You must think me loco if you think I'll swallow that one.'

'Why don't you ask the boys – what's left of them anyway?'

Chandler stared at him in silence.

Carmody met his gaze levelly.

They were alone in the small room, two battle-scarred men whose hatred for one another had destroyed their former friendship. Both wore guns. Their eyes were hard and their stances aggressive. Yet they had been talking here for half an hour without either making a threatening move. It was odd and it was uncertain. Yet each was aware that some vague hint of understanding or budding trust appeared to be intruding upon what might yet prove an explosive confrontation.

The debate continued until Marylou suddenly stepped through the doorway.

'Wes, Mr Chandler, I think you really should come. Ma says Mr Briggs may only have minutes left . . . and he does seem desperate to see you both.'

Chandler and Carmody realized Ma was right about Briggs the moment they entered the sick room. The doughty former deputy of Millertown and Whiplock under Chandler, was ashen and sinking fast, yet could still speak clearly.

'I'm sorry . . . Sheriff, Carmody,' he panted. 'You'll

never know how sorry. . . .'

'About what, man?' Chandler was still in combat mode. 'What are you talking ab—?'

'The cash shipment you left with me and Carmody that night at the jailhouse at Millertown is what, Sheriff. When it went missing, I claimed Carmody must have stolen it while I was away . . . and you believed me. Everyone believed me, including the trial judge on account I was a lawman with a good reputation over thirty years while Wes here was just something of a wild boy. So . . . so who were you and the court going to believe when I accused him. . . ?'

He broke off, coughing blood. Marylou attended to him while Carmody and Chandler traded dumbfounded looks.

The ex-sheriff of Whiplock took the dying man's hand. It felt like ice.

'You're delirious, Briggs. You've always been honest and as straight as a flagpole ever since we started—'

'I was straight until I met up with the Widow Branson, Sheriff,' Briggs cut in, his breath hoarse and rasping now. 'I fell in love for the first time in my fifty lonesome years, and the widow . . . well, she expected to be courted right, so I took to gambling to cover what I was spending and within six months I owed Slade Holder at the Can-Can more than I could earn in years. So when that night came, when the late shipment of cash came through and the bank was locked up for the weekend, meaning the jailhouse was the only place it could be held safe . . . I . . . I saw my chance, squirrelled it away, and pointed the finger at Wes here . . . and . . .'

The coughing began again. It didn't last though, and by the time Briggs had furnished every last detail covering his crime, there was no doubting the truth in every word. Both men had heard enough.

They were at the big town upriver dispatching telegraph messages to Whiplock within the hour, and two days later Chandler received the cryptic wire from the man who had replaced him as sheriff of Whiplock.

It read:

FOLLOWED YOUR INSTRUCTIONS. STOLEN BANK MONEY RECOVERED IN FULL FROM OLD WELL AT CLERMONT AS DIRECTED BY CARMODY. AWAITING FURTHER INSTRUCTIONS.

SHERIFF DUNNE

Reece Chandler was a strong man often accused of being hard. Likely he was both, but that he was a man in the truest sense of the word, Wes Carmody had no doubts on that day when, after both had read and re-read the wire from the north, Chandler turned to him in silence and extended his hand.

They shook, and their feud was over.

It was a gentler sun that spilled down over the high Mexican valley a week later. It was as though the country had put on its best face for Ma Jenner's first glimpse of the ranch bequeathed to her.

Cupped by blue hills, the valley lay green and gold before the travellers from the north as they halted on the grassy rise before the title gate. In his final letter to her, Ma's brother had told her he was leaving her 'a little piece of Paradise'.

The way straight-thinking Ma saw it, she believed she was overdue for at least some Paradise on earth after the life she'd had.

It didn't take long to open up the place and for Ma and Maylou to fix a meal from provisions they'd brought with them. Afterwards Carmody and Marylou took a stroll around the gardens then stood watching the play of sunlight over the green land.

Nothing had been decided between them. Words weren't needed; they knew where they were with one another, knew they would never be apart. What shape their lives might take from here on was unclear to Marylou. She only knew they must be together, in which case, should Carmody insist on returning to the States she would of course accompany him, although that would mean leaving Ma and Tommy.

If only Ma was not so stubborn, difficult, ornery and quick-tempered, she thought, Wes might be tempted to stay.

Then a voice reached them from within the house.

'All right, if he wants to stay on and help us get fixed – providing he keeps his hands off you . . . I guess that will be all right!'

Ma appeared, then added grudgingly, 'His friends too, I suppose. Lord knows there'll be work enough for the crowd that I can see all about me here already!'

The couple turned. Ma now stood in full view with fists on generous hips, formidable as ever yet with just the hint of a twinkle in her eye. She sniffed at her daughter's smile and gave Carmody the hard eye.

Yet she didn't withdraw the invitation.

'What do you say, darling?' Marylou asked breathlessly, squeezing his arm.

It was the big moment for Wes Carmody, a man who'd seen his share of life-changing moments over the past year. He'd known from the start he loved Marylou, but until that moment, he had been unable to envisage a future together.

Stay put down here in Old Mexico? Hang up the Colts and help whip this place into shape? Why not? The boys could stay on or drift; it would be up to them, even though he hoped they would stay.

'Well?' Ma Jenner was not renowned for her patience.

'We're staying!' Shacker called from the porch.

'Whether you do or not, Wes!' Jamie Yost added cheekily.

After a long moment, Carmody heard himself say, 'I guess that's how it will be then.'

Jamie whooped with delight and Ma went trudging back inside, half pleased and half apprehensive. She left Old Shacker gaping in surprise and pleasure at the man who was like his own son and, for the first time in their years together, he realized he was seeing Wes Carmody smile. In truth, he was grinning like a kid in the bright sunlight of Mexico as they all stood together in the bright sunlight of the San Robles land of Ma Jenner's dreams.